I0654957

Cornerstones

By David J. Kirk

Martin Sisters Publishing

Published by

Martin Sisters Publishing, LLC

www. martinsisterspublishing. com

Copyright © 2013 David J. Kirk

Martin Sisters Publishing, LLC, Kentucky.
ISBN: 978-1-62553-064-6
Mainstream/Dystopian
Printed in the United States of America
Martin Sisters Publishing, LLC

DEDICATION

For Dawne, Beth & Mitch

ACKNOWLEDGEMENTS

Linda Blakkan
Nicole Ruby Photography

Chapter 1

It was the day after we heard Washington's nose fell off that the whole mystery started to unravel. Few of us bought that wild story because we were told about it on April Fool's Day. It was Monday, April 2, 3077, early in the morning, and I was walking out to Empire Hill, when those old feelings started to return. I was the first one up. An unusually warm spring morning greeted me. I knew I had been remiss in my journal entries over the past two years, with all the babies. We actually had only two, but at times it seemed as if there were at least eight or ten of them in our small log cabin.

I jogged down the hill our cabin sat on, into the valley, then up the slope of the neighboring hill to have a chat with my old friend. "Good morning, sir. I assume all is well in the forest. I am doing well this fine spring morning. I have the best wife in the world and two great kids. The job and our business are both doing fine. Did I mention I'm finally getting my bachelor's in history next month? Tell me, then, Empire, why do I feel so incomplete?" I did not expect an answer. I walked up to brush leaves off an inlaid stone. I almost chuckled from the irony when I read the inscription:

Empire Murdock

XXXX – 3074

We couldn't even give the guy a year of birth for his grave.

I had more to think about, so I decided I needed more of a walk. I headed toward the grazing meadow.

Empire and I had shared such a childhood: homeless, parentless and penniless. My birth date was also undetermined. Oh, the orphanage gave us all one, but it was only an estimate. The military did too, if only for the reason that the Navy payroll computer wouldn't accept "unknown" in the space provided for a birth date. However, we didn't put the birth date given to him by the orphanage nor the one he received from the Marines on Murdock's grave, because neither was real.

It was about fourteen years ago when Empire, eight other boys and I, met at the Centura Orphanage. We were assigned to Delk Hall, a disgusting place that met a fitting end some years later in a yet unexplained fire. Frank Davis, Jim Donovan, Clyde Hastings, Ben Holden, Frank Miller, Albert Myers, Bo Schlitz, Corky Wall, Empire and I formed the Eagles, a brotherhood that lasts to this day. We faced a rival gang of bullies, the Mustangs. We protected each other. We grew up together, and the band became much more than a simple union. In junior high school we formed alliances with two other groups: Holy Cross and the Range. We advanced in high school and junior college, and our fights with the Mustangs became so aggressive, the school and the town soon could not distinguish the good guys from the bad guys. We were charged, tried, convicted and suddenly found ourselves running out into the wilderness to live. We then meditated, developed a strategy, and fought our way back into civilization, this time using the justice system to fight our battles. Successful, many of us then obtained college degrees; some of those advanced, and formed Anchor Farm, a limited liability corporation. We now owned four square miles of farmland and woods, raising some livestock, crops, and organic vegetables.

Many of us were gone, though. Jim Donovan had finished college, moved to Atlanta, became a lobbyist, and had married. Frank Davis became a lawyer and moved down South also. Empire joined the Marines and was killed in a motor vehicle accident in Mobile.

I approached the meadow that had been fenced in for cattle grazing, and sang to the cows. "Saa boss, saa boss ... Saa hey oh, boss." Two jet black Angus heifers came trotting to the fence in front of me. I have this odd knack for calling cows - a local phenomenon, if you will. Our farming neighbor, Milt Frazer, used to have me call in his escaped cattle when he didn't feel like chasing after them. It only worked with cows, never pigs or chickens. My 'spell' never lasted long, because after about half a minute my two bovine friends snorted, then walked slowly back toward the barn.

Traveller, our white Siberian husky, then joined me. The dog was the common pet of our little community, so he had a lot of ground to cover. He hoisted his two front legs up on the fence, looked at the cows, and then at me. I said, "Everything's fine here, Trav." He jumped down and scampered off. This had probably been just a brief stop on his early morning rounds. He seemed to believe that he had to keep track of everything that happened on our large grounds. He wandered a lot. That's why we named him after General Lee's horse.

I walked back toward my house admiring the budding trees and the warm, fresh air. It had been a mild winter and a dry spring. The vegetables would be planted soon and our garden would be greening up. I loved the garden in spring, before the chores of weed pulling and watering began.

Ascending the hill our cabin sat on, I saw my wife, Marie, sitting in her wooden chaise lounge sipping coffee. A steaming cup sat on the arm of the empty chair next to her. She smiled; I kissed her, then sat and dove into my coffee.

"You've been up to Empire Hill already this morning I see," Marie said.

My pretty wife smiled at me. She was absolutely the best decision I had made in my whole life. I met her through her brother, who was a member of our affiliate club, Holy Cross. They were a group of devout naturalists, and she tagged along with her brother. Her experience being his 'tag-along' had turned her into a whiz of a horticulturalist. She and her friends helped us start our organic produce business. Also a registered nurse, she had worked at the orphanage where I grew up, until the economy tanked and she was laid off. She now did a few midnight shifts each week at the military hospital at the local military base. I adored Marie; she was organized, rational, and resilient.

"Yeah, I said good morning to Empire, and then took a walk to the meadow to see the cows. I saw Traveller down there."

"Oh, yeah? How is he? Did you tell him to come visit me?"

"I didn't have a chance before he split. Darn dog has a schedule to keep!"

"What do you have going on today?"

"Oh, a couple of service calls this morning, and then I have that senior history seminar this afternoon. I should be home early."

Down the hill about fifty yards, Angie Holden came out of her cabin. Her husband, Ben, followed close behind her. Ben Holden was our group leader and manager of our company.

His great height and large frame dwarfed Angie, who's barely five foot tall. She had dated Ben since early high school and was like a little sister to all of us. Being a 'small package' but a 'big handful', anyone wanting to get into an argument with her would definitely be in for a long day. We soon heard her yelling at Ben about some potted plant sitting on the deck. He finally threw up his hands and went back in the house.

I smiled at Marie; "Dare me to get something started?"

"Don't do it, Dan. You'll regret it."

I cupped my hands around my mouth. "Hey, Angie!"

She looked up, but couldn't see us too well through the branches of an evergreen tree.

"We've got babies sleeping up here. How about giving that big trap of yours a rest?"

She looked again but was still having trouble locating us. "That you, Kelley?" She raised her fist in the air, "How 'bout you come down here and say that to my face? I'll drop you like a bad habit, boy." Then her tone softened, "Hey, Dan, is Marie up there?"

"Here, Angie," Marie yelled back.

"Do you think you can come down later and check out my plant? I think Ben's killing it."

"Okay."

"Oh, Marie," Angie went on, "sorry about that loser of a husband you had to settle for. You could have done a lot better."

"I know; I felt sorry for him."

Angie went back in and Marie laughed, "I told you there's no winning an argument with her, but you guys keep trying."

I walked over to the machine shed after getting ready for work. My old diesel truck was still puttering along after several years of customer calls. Still working for Ron's Electrical, I began to work into being his partner. He allowed me to slowly earn a percentage, handing off customers to me, while he began a slowdown toward retirement. In a few years I would own the company and he would work for me on a part-time basis.

My two service calls that morning were less than challenging. The first was merely installing a new breaker and the second was me scolding a guy for having too many high usage appliances plugged into his extension cord.

I finished early, and then drove up to the university on the east side of Centura. The high school, tech school, and college were all on one big campus on a peninsula that stuck out into Lake Michigan. I stopped at a burger joint I had frequented as a teenager, ordered lunch to go, and ate it on the drive. The stiff breeze that was blowing in off the lake reminded me that it wasn't summer yet.

I was finishing up the work for my history degree online, but the senior seminar held monthly residential classes at the facility. I was a few minutes early, so I perused the bulletin boards in the Humanities Department student lounge. Something caught my eye.

I read a poster that announced "'Marvelous' Marvin Greene – Nationally Renowned God-based Motivational Speaker, Student Union Assembly Hall, One Night Only!" I almost lost my burger right there on the spot. The Marv Greene from my teen years was a different character altogether. President of the famed 'Mustangs', Marv oversaw a gang of bullies and extortionists who had ravaged the Southside of Centura and the orphanage where I grew up. One of his goons killed a roommate of mine. Others beat up Frank Davis and Clyde Hastings, and even threatened Frank's sister. I personally experienced two black eyes from those creeps. Marv resigned his membership in the gang shortly after the homicide, and promoted a big sob story about being a 'forgiven sinner' and the victim of a cruel society. Most of it proved to be lies. We found out he came from a very well-off family. After a while, he began to notice the effect his story had on people, and he was soon filling rooms to listen to his phony tales of redemption. After moving down South, Marv Greene realized he could make money at this. His "God-based" claim was questionable, especially since he was not an ordained minister. Nevertheless, there were rumors of faith healings and speaking in tongues.

As I was humoring myself with thoughts of attending his seminar and throwing tomatoes, the clock struck ten to the hour and the classrooms emptied into the lounge. Then I heard a yell from down the hall.

"Kelley. Dan Kelley. The magic number is two, Mr. Kelley."

I wheeled around to see Dr. Phillips, chairman of the electrical engineering department. I was hoping to avoid him.

He came right up to me, his raised hand holding up two fingers, "Two, that is the number, sir. With your military training, your associate's degree in electricity and the engineering courses you've taken so far, I could get you a B.S. in engineering with just two semesters, not that crap history degree you're going to get. We could start over the summer; I could then take you into the master's program. One year after that, Mr. Kelley, and you could have an M.S. in electrical engineering."

"But I like history, Dr. Phillips. Thanks anyway."

"Do you know you have a 4.0 grade point average right now? Do you know there were only six students in the last decade to do that? Do you know who the last one was?"

"Che Guevara?"

"Very funny. No. It was Dr. Albert Myers, your business partner. And he's in mathematics, Mr. Kelley. That's science. History is speculative, hearsay, stories, and conjecture. Tell me, how smart are you? What's your secret?"

"No secret, sir. I learned it in the first grade: read the assignments, do the homework, hand in the papers, study for the tests. Simple."

"You see? It's about applying yourself. If carrying a 4.0 average was that simple, everyone would be doing it. I don't believe in IQ, Mr. Kelley. Some idiot psychologist thought that up. It's all in the application. I want you in my program."

"I'm fine with the technical side of electricity."

"You could be designing satellite systems. Right now you're running wires through walls."

"I'm interested in history," I said, not sounding too sure of myself.

"I've been watching you lately," he went on. "I am getting the feeling that you're not too interested in anything right now."

"That's not true."

"And I think I know why. It's taken you eight years to get your bachelor's. You sit around that stupid campfire in the woods down south with your 'awareness' group and talk about the meaning of life and the world is passing you by. Plus, you got that crackpot, Dr. Thomas Pine, telling you about Aristotle and Plato and Pirsig and the 'higher meaning' of things and all assorted other cow manure."

He was getting a little closer to setting me off.

"And what about your family, Mr. Kelley? How are you looking out for their future? Are you going to teach your kids how to slop the hogs or are you going to send them to top universities? Do you know how much money you could...?"

I snapped. "All right. You can insult my job, my major, and my friends all you want. But don't ever tell me how to take care of my family! I'm doing just fine with that, okay?"

Phillips just stood there staring at me with his mouth open. I gazed around to see all the students looking at us. Then I saw Dr. Principi standing in the doorway of his classroom, leaning on his walker.

"Trying to recruit my students, Dr. Phillips?"

The engineer just turned and took off down the hall, then yelled, "I want you, Mr. Kelley."

I brushed past Principi without saying a word and sat down. I saw that I had joined the entire graduating class of history majors, all four of us.

Dr. Principi slowly dragged himself to his podium. He was amazing. He started out teaching high school, and then moved into the college ranks by simply waiting everyone out. He wasn't that old. He only appeared old because of his crippled condition. He was a masterful teacher. They couldn't fire him and found few reasons not to promote him. He earned his Ph.D. and was soon teaching higher level college classes and some in the graduate school. However, his department was shrinking because history had only one classroom. The humanities and social sciences were taking an enrollment beating because of society's drastic need for scientists. Large corporations and the Federal Government were even paying high stipends for students to go into such occupations. We were a high-tech nation who didn't know how to have fun.

Our professor cleared his throat. "Okay, now that all the fireworks are over, welcome to our last class meeting. The four of you form this year's graduating class of Bachelor of Arts, History. This is your senior seminar for making some sense of all the dates you memorized."

I heard some chuckles.

"In this course we discussed four major eras: prehistory through the Romans, post-Roman (The Medieval and Modern Eras), 'Old World' (The Post-Modern Era), and our 'New World'. Today we talk about the New World and how it differs from the first three. Let's first review some events.

"Around 2110, we experienced devastating climate change, a mini-ice age if you will. It lasted for several centuries. Now commonly named the 'Youngest Dryas', the event caused the population of the world, and this country, to abandon the high latitudes and cram into the global areas that were close to the equator. This population shift, beginning around 2114, began a decade-long state of civil disruption, now called 'The Chaos'. However, a rogue biotech accident in 2126 caused the spread of a plague that killed about ninety percent of the population. There are stories that the military had to bulldoze acres of valuable cropland in order to dig mass graves. The identities of the victims were lost in the confusion.

"The 'Great Thaw' around 2700 caused the 'Youngest Dryas' to loosen its grip on the north, although our country never again regained the population to resettle the abandoned areas. Now, the people of the world, the U.S. included, inhabit small pockets of areas that are able to support them. The map showing the country at this time includes what's left of eleven states in the southeast. The remaining land area reverted to territorial status. This is why two-thirds of the country is now uninhabited wilderness.

"Of local interest, in 2950, national security concerns motivated the government to create isolated military outposts throughout the land in order to protect our uninhabited areas from foreign threats. No other countries ever had the manpower or the will to do such a thing, but we paranoid Americans felt fear anyway. Bases were constructed on Long Island, here in the Midwest, San Antonio and Southern California. These bases had no land connection with civilization, and still don't, and must be resupplied by air.

"Thompson Defense Base was placed here on Lake Michigan, between the now nonexistent cities of Chicago and Milwaukee, which were leveled by the glaciers, primarily because of small amounts of coal and oil nearby. It houses detachments of the all the military departments, has an airstrip, and a harbor to base a small flotilla of naval vessels. The town, now city, of Centura grew around it to provide support for the base.

"But to our topic. What did we learn, or didn't we learn, from this drastic historical shift?"

The young lady next to me spoke up. "At the end of the 'Old World', we were assaulting our resources. 'The Chaos' and 'The Plague' reduced demand tremendously, but we still have not made the conversion to sustainable fuels. The air and water quality in the states we have re-populated has not improved that much."

"The Arts went into a coma," a gentleman at the back of the class added, "and have not fully recovered. Art, music, dance, drama, even movies, are digital remakes from the 'Old World'.

Atlanta and Miami have the only two symphonies in the United States. We have eight major league baseball teams and six football teams. People are still listening to remastered Bob Dylan recordings. I mean he was the greatest and all, but the music world is now static."

I loved this class. By the senior year, all the skeptics and the disinterested had been weeded out. Gone were the "I'm in this class 'cause my Mommy says I have to go to college and make something out of myself," folks. There were five historians in that room.

I said, "We forgot how to laugh. Old World standup comics were one of the last free art forms. They had a license to laugh at people, laugh at themselves, and laugh at our sacred institutions. We were, and in some cases still are, too focused on survival that we devalued our sense of humor and what it can do for us. That was the only thing that separated us from the other mammals."

A lively discussion ensued but the class' enthusiasm was drying up after these final two hours. As if they were all first semester freshman, the lovely spring day beaconed through the windows.

Dr. Principi thanked us for our participation. "See all of you who are coming for graduation and again next fall. Oh, and I'd like to see Mr. Kelley after class."

The girl next to me teased, "Aw, in trouble again, Dan? She smiled. "Have a good summer."

"You too, Sara."

The professor walked out from behind his lectern and leaned on the front of his desk, "I heard Dr. Phillips discussing the benefits of an engineering degree with you before class."

"Yeah, he certainly has an odd way of recruiting students."

"Sean Phillips is the back end of a horse." He gave me a knowing wink. "I've known him for years; he's always been that way. It's not bothering you, is it?"

"Oh no, I'm use to him and people like him."

"You could still do what he suggested, take his courses and then get a double major. You have all the math and science you'd need."

"Get a double in engineering and history? Both disciplines would try me for being a heretic. No, I have absolutely no need to ever talk to Dr. Phillips again."

"But, you're interested in history, right?"

"Yes, sir."

"Yet, I don't have your application for the master's program. How come?"

"I'm not sure I'm going to start in the fall. I'm ... having some 'ambition issues'."

He sighed, "Well, I don't want you here if your whole heart is not in it. But Phillips did make a point. You're twenty-six, Dan. With an M.A. and the grades you earn, I'm sure you could get on the faculty here. However, they don't hire too many forty-year-olds, so don't wait too long. I get the feeling, though, that this isn't an 'ambition problem'."

"What then?"

"I think it's a distraction problem. It may even be related to that talk we had when you were in the seventh grade."

"Oh, that thing with my parents? That reached a dead-end years ago, Dr. P. It's an unsolvable problem." I realized my error in making that statement as soon as it came out.

"Well now. That is not something a summa cum laude graduate says, Mr. Kelley, especially one of mine. Okay, you can see by the size of this class, there is no way all the slots are going to be filled. You can file anytime. However, take some time and get this mess figured out. Gee, you have that gang of eggheads down there. Use them. And of course, you have full access to my private library anytime you want it. Oh, are you coming to graduation?"

"Probably not."

"Sorry that you did not get elected valedictorian. That 'whiz' over in chemistry almost tied your GPA and is a full-time student. And I'm sure it was people like Dr. Phillips who just couldn't stand a humanities student giving that speech."

"No worries. I'm not much on that speech stuff anyway. See you soon, sir."

When I entered the cab of my truck and hit the fonapp of my handcomp, flashing lights informed me of several emergency service calls and dashed all hopes I had of getting home early.

It was dusk when I walked up the hill toward our cabin.

Marie was seated in her chair next to the big oak tree, feeding our one-year-old, Patrick, out of a jar while little Annie was in a heated game of badminton with Bo Schlitz. They weren't using the net, too high for her, but just volleying back and forth.

"Hey, Annie, come give me a hug," I yelled to her.

She ignored me, too engrossed.

"Hey, what are you playing?"

"Battem," she mispronounced.

I sat next to Marie, and she asked, "Get them all done?"

"Yeah, they took a while but weren't too complicated. You did get my message about dinner, I take it?"

"Yes," she answered, smiling at me, "one of your customers is grilling steak and offers you one? I'm sure you did everything you could to refuse. Okay, that's your second red meat of the week, so no more."

"I should have lied and said they were having tuna." I picked up Pat and held him. "Bo seems to be doing well."

"Yeah, if he keeps on the medication. Annie sure likes him."

Annie and Bo were done playing, but they were involved in an intense discussion.

Then my wife said, "Annie, let's go in, honey. It's getting late."

The little girl came running up to us and I finally got a belated hug. She then pointed up toward our cabin and said, "Home."

I nodded in agreement.

I handed Pat to Marie. "I'll be in soon, I'm gonna talk to Bo."

I sat and watched my friend gather up the badminton equipment. Bo Schlitz, one of the ten original Eagles, developed some severe mental health issues by the time he had reached young adulthood. He started experiencing psychotic episodes and was hospitalized for over three months. Bo struggled. After he received an emergency medical technician certificate, he was temporarily hired as a civilian paramedic with the military ambulance service. However, when active duty personnel were available, he was laid off. He tried to join the military, but was rejected due to his illness. Then he got a bachelor's of science in nursing, but couldn't get a license to practice for the same reason. He just couldn't get a break. He now worked for our LLC, but we sure kept a close eye on him.

When he walked toward me, I waved.

"Bo, how goes it?"

"Fine." Bo stood before me but made no attempt to sit down. He seemed to be sweating a little more than usual for playing badminton with a two-year-old. "Sorry, I'm a little sweaty. I was out running just before your daughter wanted to play. I was telling her a story. She sure is a little sweetheart, Dan."

"Yes, she is. So, how many more tomato plants are going in this year?"

"Your wife and Angie told me they wanted to do another half-acre. I dunno, we're pretty stretched already with watering and weeding."

"I think their eyes are bigger than our brawn."

"You got that right. Well, Dan, I need a shower and to do some reading. See ya later."

Bo headed up to the little horseshoe ridge where we built our first bunkhouse years ago. Bo and Corky Wall were both still single, and lived there.

I headed for the cabin.

Marie was bathing Patrick and I found Annie, clad in her ankle length night gown, out on the south porch. She was making a poor attempt at picking up her toys and putting them in a box.

Annie looked up at me with that big smile, knowing full well she had me wrapped around her little finger. She pointed out to a tall pine tree southeast of the house and said, "Home."

"Home?" I kneeled down in front of her. "This is home," I pointed down. "That's a tree - home to birdies."

"Home."

"Home is that tree? Who told you that?"

"Bo."

"Bo means a birdie's home. But do you know what our home has?"

"What?"

"Ice cream."

"ICE CEAM!"

As I dished out her treat, my daughter did her famous ice cream dance. She was so crazy for the stuff, she would stand by the counter next to me and dance with delight. Ice cream was her 'heaven on earth'.

Annie was standing in front of the coffee table, eating her treat, while I watched a satellite news channel.

Her mom came in and sighed, putting her hands on her hips. "Annie!"

"Ice ceam."

"Yes, I know, young lady. Did you happen to tell your daddy that you had ice cream when you first came in the house?"

"Ice ceam," she repeated. Then my sheepish little friend took advantage of her Fifth Amendment rights and clammed up. When mom left again to check on Pat, she looked at me and smiled. I admired my little girl's philosophy. The next time I'm asked some deep question, like, "What is the meaning of life?" I'm going to respond, "Ice ceam."

After tuck-ins and stories and songs, I returned to my news program. Marie was in the kitchen when I called to her, "Hon, do you think I should be an electrical engineer?"

She joined me on the couch, "Has Dr. Phillips been after you again?"

"I mean, think how much money we could make. I could get you nicer things."

She took my hand and looked me right in the eye, "We've been over this about fifty times already. I like it here. Our families are here, your business is growing. The LLC is finally paying out, and I have my job. We're doing okay. I have a family of squirrels that sit on the windowsill over the kitchen sink and wait for me to feed them lunch every day. I want my kids to know woods and prairies and animals. What do you want to do, live on the tenth floor of a high-rise in town, and have the kids get in fights on the way home from school?"

"No, not really."

"If you like electricity AND history, then do them both", she said resignedly, shrugging and wrinkling up her cute nose.

We sat and watched the news for a while. I said, "So, it looks like that story is true."

"Yeah."

We were watching a story on the news that was showing a reconnaissance video made by a military drone out in the vast uninhabited West. It had dipped low to get a shot of Mount Rushmore to reveal that old George's nose had indeed finally fallen off, rendering all four images on the monument unrecognizable.

Chapter 2

The next Sunday afternoon, a few of the Eagles and Tom Pine, our mentor and resident genealogy expert, held our quarterly conference, in which we discuss searches for missing relatives. Some members showed interest in finding relatives, while others wanted to leave well enough alone. Orphans hold grudges and some of us had been either mistreated or abandoned by family members. Success varied. We were able to locate Clyde Hastings' mother, unfortunately deceased, and did get him connected with his sister. Jim Donavon's mom, a prostitute who left him at a hospital as an infant, was in a prison down South. We holofaxed Jim the information but never heard if he did anything with it. My parents' disappearance out on the prairie was probably the most notorious case, but we had progressed very little in the last eight years and had not even discussed it for months.

I was the first to arrive, and watched the others come into our newly built addition to the Anchor Farms machine shop. Our 'Eagles brother', Dr. Albert Myers, a professor of mathematics at the university, was the first to arrive. Al had two masters' degrees and a doctorate before he was twenty-two. Since he was an honest to goodness 'genius', we all thought Al should be off on worldwide tours, giving lectures, but he stuck with his orphan buddies. He had based his dissertation entitled "O'Dea's Riddle" on my father.

Dr. Thomas Pine, Chair of the Department of Philosophy at the college, was not an 'Eagle' but more of a 'guiding light' to the group. He still attended our Saturday-night-around-the campfire philosophy sessions. Tom had his trusty pipe in his mouth.

Dr. Phillips had been right; it was an 'awareness' group, a therapy session, and a general discussion venue where many of us worked out hard feelings. Dr. Pine and his wife Diane, a childhood friend of mine, stayed over at the Holden's on the weekends when we held these meetings.

Quiet Frank Miller, an accomplished author, came in next. His book, Living on the Prairie, was about my Dad also, only from a more human level. Frank lived in Centura and wrote articles for scholarly journals over the Compunet.

A former hunting and trapping guide for our company, Clyde Hastings had traded in his gun for a camera. He now shot wildlife photos and had several printed in some popular magazines. He loved the woods and wildlife and spent a great deal of time outdoors with his girlfriend, Mary. Clyde was quiet, but had an incredible knack for seeming to be right in his impressions. If the rest of us came to impasse, he was our tiebreaker.

Al Myers stood, laid his handcomp on the table, and projected holoscreen for his slides. Al ran the meetings and did his best to keep the discussions within scientific guidelines. I sometimes found his insistence on only considering conclusions based on provable facts a bit constricting. He was obviously a 'child' of his discipline.

Al gave Dr. Pine a sour look and said, "Tom, you're not going to smoke that thing in here, are you?"

"The first time you say something stupid, Al, I'm lighting up."

Al looked at me and asked, "Where's Schlitz?"

"Beats me, I emessaged him about the meeting," I responded.

"He's on a lot of 'meds'," Tom Pine added, "and could be napping."

"Okay," Al went on, "Where were we? I think we finished the last meeting with Clyde Hastings' sister. Is that okay, Clyde?"

"Great. Thanks."

"How about we take a look at Kelley's thing?" Frank Miller said, "We haven't gone over that for a while. Can you do the summary, Al?"

"Okay. Wait; let me pull it up on the screen here. Okay, well, we all know Patrick O'Dea, wife Lilly, and son, Patrick, Jr., travelled to an isolated outpost in Illinois Territory, date unknown, just across the river from the site of Old St. Louis. This site was established by Leap Frog Technologies, and was primarily a base for expeditions into the wilderness. Leap Frog had contracts with the Federal Government to retrieve certain materials, designated classified, from the uninhabited territories to the west and north of that site. These items were buried during the 'Youngest Dryas'. Although they had government contracts, it was a completely civilian enterprise.

"O'Dea worked as a general laborer, handyman, mechanic, and cared for the company cattle herd. Around 3049 or 50, young Dan here was born, and it was indeed a dark day in history."

I 'booed', and grinned.

"Delivered by a midwife, there was no registration of his birth. In August 3055, for some unknown reason, Mr. O'Dea packed his family in a UXU amphibious vehicle and took off across the prairie in a general northeast direction. How he got this vehicle is still unknown. Where and why is also unknown.

"Now to the puzzle. Patrick did not know where he was going. He meandered through the country in a confused manner. He did appear, at times, to be heading in a general direction, and then stopped for two or three days in a specific location. We assumed these stops were to hunt for food, recharge the solar batteries for the electric motor, rest, or a combination of these reasons. He made four of these extended stops, and you can see by the map on the wall, we have called these 'Destinations A thorough D'. We know this because the integrated A.I. in his vehicle left a record of his route. But you can see, the travel lines between these destinations are erratic, some even crossing back over previously traveled routes.

"Then it gets interesting. While the family was headed to what we have specified as 'Destination E' in early September 3055, the vehicle broke down a mere two miles or so short of his goal. With a snowstorm approaching, both parents left the vehicle, never to return. Patrick, and Dan, ages six and four, respectively, became scared. After getting out to relieve themselves, the boys became separated in the snowstorm. A rescue helicopter picked up Dan later that evening, completely missing Patrick, Jr. who a day or two later started wandering back toward Old St. Louis and was picked up by Leap Frog employees. The rest we know.

"Of note, on April 17, 3056, the Mississippi River flooded and wiped out most of the Leap Frog settlement, their records, and drowned most of the inhabitants.

"In the summer of 3070, after receiving information from Dan's newly discovered brother, Pat Jr., we made an expedition to the site, about 125 miles south of here. We found the vehicle, broken down, with the left trak severed, and most of the solarskin missing. We assumed that is why Patrick, Sr. and his wife left the boys; however, we don't have any proof of that. We also found the coordinates to 'Destination E' scratched into the cowl of the Amphibitrak. After hiking to Destination E, only a couple of miles north, we only found three oak trees and an 'Old World' house foundation. There appeared to be nothing significant about Destination E to justify such a perilous journey.

"Our mystery still includes: 1) Why did O'Dea leave Old St. Louis? 2) Why the erratic route? 3) If he had the coordinates to 'Destination E', why didn't he just go straight there? 4) Why did he leave two little boys alone? and 5) What happened to the couple? We've been scratching our heads for years."

"I have something to add," Frank Miller said. "I have a friend who works for the Occupational Safety and Health Administration. We were shooting the bull the other day and he told me he found an old report on this Leap Frog place. Seems like we have someone around who maybe can help."

"Who?"

"Do you guys remember Marv Greene?"

Tom Pine huffed, "You mean the self-appointed 'savior of the masses'? The 'motivational evangelist'?"

"Yeah, his dad was there."

"He was an engineer, right?"

"Yep. He used to be in the Army. Not sure when and how long he was there."

Al asked, "Anyone want to follow up on this?"

I raised my hand.

Al went on, "Pending Dan's response on this item, in our last meeting we considered closing out this case. Do we want to put this to a vote?"

Tom Pine made a gesture as if he was attempting to light his pipe and said, "My vote depends on how Dan feels about this." He looked at me, "Dan, you used to be obsessed with solving this puzzle, but in this meeting so far, and the last few months in general, you have shown little enthusiasm. How do you feel?"

"Mixed," I said, "or mixed up, would be a better term. I sometimes think I would be better off, as well as my family and friends, if I would just accept this situation as unexplainable and move on. My teachers are getting on my case; my wife says I'm aloof. I've got to drop this victim-orphan thing and just get on with my life. I have a lot going for me, and I'm wasting a lot of valuable resources here."

"I complain a lot about our lack of facts in this case, Dan," Al spoke up, "but I've never once considered any of this a waste of time."

Miller added, "You would do all this and more for any of us."

Clyde Hastings summarized, "Dan, when I was in the Army, my combat instructor yelled and screamed and drilled one fact in our heads: We don't leave anyone, dead or alive, out on the field. We take everyone home. You, and now it's we, have two people out there, and we're going to get them."

After the meeting I caught up with Clyde, who was heading toward the woods with his camera. "Clyde, thanks for that, I guess."

He sighed, "Sometimes, 'Mr. Straight-A-Smarty-Pants', you confuse me. A waste of time? I don't mean to be sappy here, but do you remember teaching Empire how to read? Do you remember how Corky, in the seventh grade, couldn't pass third grade math until you and Davis tutored him? Both those guys got through high school because of you two. Remember?"

"That was easy for me; that was nothing."

"Then let your friends help you with what comes easy for them."

"But Marie says …"

"I know what Marie says. She's talked to me about this. Do you think you're fooling her about going up on Empire Hill to say Hi! to Murdock? She sees you. She watches you look over the tree line. You're looking down south about a hundred miles, aren't you, Dan? Your heart and mind are down there on that prairie, and she wants both back home. Now go see Mr. Greene, and let me know what you find out. If this doesn't pan out we'll try something else."

On the afternoon of the next day, I was up on the Northside of Centura following my GPSbot to the elder Greene's residence. I pulled up in front of an impressive stone-walled, two story house. The whole property was enclosed by a wrought-iron fence with a locked gate. I pulled my hood over my head to protect me from the pouring rain, walked up, and rang the bell. A stately gentleman in a white coat opened the front door and yelled, "Sorry, we didn't call an electrician."

"I know. I'm not here for that. I was wondering if I can speak to Mr. Greene."

"Do you know him?"

"No, but I have to speak with him about a personal matter."

"I'm sorry; he doesn't see anyone he doesn't know. I suggest you send an emessage explaining who you are and what the nature of your business is."

"I did that yesterday, he didn't respond."

"Sorry." He shut the door quickly.

I drove to a sandwich shop a few blocks away, got some lunch, and sat down to call Clyde. The screen on my handcomp showed Hastings in the image room of his cabin. Corky Wall was with him. "Hey Clyde, Greene wouldn't see me."

"Why not?"

"His butler said it was because he didn't know me."

Corky looked over Clyde's shoulder, interrupting, "Hey, Kelley, what are you eating?"

"Genovine meatball sandwich." It was just like beef, but was cruelty-free.

"Really? Don't let your wife or Angie Holden find out about that. Those vegan fascists are out to kill all of us, Dan. Get that sandwich to go and make a run for it." He shot me a crooked grin.

I just shook my head. Sometimes Corky spoke as if he was from the 'Old World'.

Clyde continued, "Dan, we need to try another tactic. Why don't we try talking to Marv?"

"'Marvelous' Marv?"

"Yeah, he's speaking at the college."

"That doesn't mean we'll get to talk to him."

"No, but if we had backstage passes the chances would be better."

"How do we get those?"

"Your old high school sweetheart, Lisa Richardson. She's an events planner and PR person for the university. Work your magic."

"And bring me back a spicy sausage with green pepper and onions," Cork added, "and sneak it past the 'guards'." I could see Traveller following me the whole way to his place.

The rain showed no sign of letting up when I drove out to the university campus. After wading through the parking lot, I made my way to the administration offices. Lisa sat alone in her cubicle, still wearing those dark framed eyeglasses. "Lady, you call an electrician?"

She looked up, smiled, and said, "Dan Kelley? I haven't seen you in ages." She came over and gave me a big hug. "Have a seat." She returned behind her desk. "So, look at you, married with two babies! I ran in to your wife over at the School of Nursing a couple times. Very lovely girl, too good for you by the way." This was getting to be a common theme.

"Well, she felt sorry for me." I recalled the exchange with Angie, with some amusement.

"And the kids?"

"A girl and boy, two and one."

"Wow. And you're a master electrician. But hey, your GPA is getting talked about a lot around here. I hear the graduate programs are fighting over you. Make any decisions yet?"

"I was thinking of changing over to animal husbandry."

She looked at me oddly.

I added, "It's a joke."

"Oh, sorry, for a minute, I forgot how weird you can get."

"So what's up with you? Find a man yet?"

"No, but thanks for bringing that up. Hey, what's that dreamboat friend of yours, Frank, up to?"

"Davis? He moved to Florida a long time ago. He got married last year."

"No. Not that dull lawyer. The writer, Frank Miller."

"He's still writing away."

"Is he dating anyone special?"

"I don't know. He was kind of steady with some girl, but I haven't seen her around lately. I thought you were living with some fisherman."

"Naw. Broke up. I moved home last year -needed the money to finish working on a master's. So, Dan, what can I do for you?"

"I need a favor."

"Figures."

"I need two backstage passes to the Marv Greene presentation."

She looked at me oddly again and said, "Marv Greene? You? You don't seem like the type."

"I'm not interested in his message; it's to do with my parents."

Lisa reached into a file cabinet behind her and retrieved two passes. She held them up in the air. "I'll make ya a deal. I'll give you these two passes if you set me up with Frank Miller."

"Geeze, Lisa. He hates when I do that."

"Come on, Dan, don't be a 'poop'. Help a poor girl out here."

"So no date, no passes?"

"Oh!" She threw them down on the desk in front of me. "I would have given them to you anyway. I was just hoping."

"Okay, okay. I'll see what I can do."

"Just one date. He doesn't have to fall madly in love with me, but I know he will."

"Thanks, Lisa," I stood and headed out.

"Oh, Dan?"

"What?

"Those two kids of yours got lucky, ya know? Having you for a dad and all."

"Thank you, Lisa."

The compliment was a much-needed end to a rainy and frustrating day

I was perfectly happy doing jobs near my home. When Ron suggested we start taking on more Northside calls, I thought we would rake in the dough. However, it appeared that I spent more time and gas driving around switching on tripped breakers or changing light bulbs. I came to the conclusion that rich people are incredibly cheap. They seemed to be the first ones to forgo the more expensive fixes that would save them money in the long run, for a band-aid approach. Of course, that was probably why they were rich. The moderately rich were that way, but people with money like Mr. Greene appeared to have didn't hire small time electricians like me.

On the evening of April 18th, Clyde and I attended the revival. Perhaps our prejudices caused us to underestimate Marv Greene's popularity, but the student union hall was packed. We stood near the doors in the back. This allowed my partner to mutter profanities and walk out every ten minutes or so at what he considered insincerity in Marv's presentation.

'Marvelous' Marv could work a crowd, that much was sure. He was insightful, made interesting points with logical support, and could get the audience roaring with laughter with his well-timed jokes. I didn't hear any extreme examples of evangelicalism. He spoke more about moral community and the need to help others. Since events of the past isolated cultures into small pockets around the globe, people seemed to forget about the value of altruism. It was, however, primarily an academic crowd, so Marv may have modified his speech to fit his audience.

After the presentation, we waited in a conference room adjacent to Marv's dressing room with about a dozen or so others.

A young blonde woman, impeccably dressed and holding a clipboard, walked into the center and announced, "Marvin is on a tight travel schedule, so unfortunately he will not be doing autographs or receive well-wishers. However, all those who are willing to accept Jesus Christ as their Lord and Savior, please line up here. He will be with you shortly."

Clyde and I looked at each other, and then moved in front of Marv's dressing room door.

Only one person was ahead of us, a young girl clutching her program to her chest and staring up at the ceiling with a smile on her face. She turned to Clyde and said, "He is here."

"He is," Clyde responded, and then looking at me said, "I've always wanted to be in this line."

"Now, don't blaspheme, Hastings," I responded.

The young lady came out after only a minute or two, with that same dreamy look on her face. Then Clyde and I entered. Marv was standing in the middle of the room, staring at us. He had removed his jacket and tie and was wiping sweat off his face with a towel.

I approached and held out my hand, "Hi Marv, I'm Dan ..."

"I know who you are," shaking my hand and then extended his to Clyde.

Hastings did not reciprocate.

"So, Dan Kelley, I take it you two are not here to be saved."

"No, I was saved years ago. Not too sure about my friend here."

I began to fear we were going to have a problem with Clyde.

"So, Marv, how's the 'savior' business?" Clyde asked.

"I don't save people, Mr. Hastings. I merely refer them to appropriate clergy."

"Funny, I had a visit from some of your clergy a few years ago, back in my dorm room at Delk Hall. Remember them? They worked me over pretty good. They also worked over a guy named Governor Viche, too, I recall."

"I didn't order that, Clyde. That was Bus Quint. I was associated with a bad crowd. I have begged forgiveness from the Lord for those days, and I was given it. Perhaps you should do the same for your rage."

"Perhaps you should go shovel your insincere baloney down south, away from people who have different memories of those days!"

Marv walked over to a chair, "Dan, you can stay, but your friend will have to leave."

"I think ..."

Clyde raised his hand to stop me, "No, Dan. I'll leave. You've got bigger fish to fry. This is not why we're here." He walked out of the room.

Marv turned to look at me, "I didn't order that hit on Viche."

"I know, Marv. I know that. You'll have to excuse Clyde; his dad was beating him up before he could walk. After his family dumped him in an alley, society took over. Things run real deep in him."

"And I suppose the Mustangs and I didn't help either." He looked me right in the eye and said, "I'm very sorry for all that, Dan, and what we did to you."

"Okay."

"So, what can I do for you?"

"I want to talk to your dad."

"So, write him an email."

"I already did; he won't see me."

"What do you want to talk to him about?"

"I'm looking for information on my parents. They were at that private recovery site at Old St. Louis. I heard your dad was there."

"I think he was, early in his career. He doesn't like to talk about that much. And this is about your parents? I read Miller's book, Living on the Prairie. Interesting. I'm sure he would be willing to help a guy locate his parents. I'll speak to him. I'm staying there tonight."

"Thanks, Marv. Hey, can I ask you one thing about the old days? Why did you resign from the Mustangs so quickly?"

He looked at me and smiled, "Why, it was you."

"Me?"

"You. You and the Eagles. You fought so darn well. You fought us all."

"Marv, we were ten scrawny seventh graders. You numbered at least thirty. You guys were high school age and even older."

He chuckled and then went on, "I don't mean to make light, Dan, but your ignorance of the old days surprises me. We didn't have gang fights. We didn't fight at all. I was a rich kid with too much time on his hands and too little to do. The gang was my excitement. We took kids lunch money; can you believe that? Psyche building was all we did. Dan, an enemy doesn't fear you for what you'll do to him, he fears you for what he thinks you will do to him. We didn't have to actually hit anyone. It was a facade, a rumor. We stood around on street corners, in our colors, with our fists clenched. Funny, I don't even remember what our colors were."

"But the Eagles didn't exactly strike fear in the hearts of people."

"No. You did much more than that. Dan, we once had a family dog. One day a momma raccoon and her youngsters stopped for a nap in our tool shed. Our dog decided to clear them out of his territory. Tell me, do you know what a momma raccoon does when her and her cubs are cornered?"

"Well, I'm a little more familiar with black bears, but I get the picture."

"That dog barely survived. It was at the vet's for two and a half months before he was well enough to come home. When you guys lined up in that yard behind Delk Hall, and charged us, do you know how ridiculous you looked? These ten little thirteen and fourteen year olds came scampering across the grass at us. We laughed. Then something happened. Corky Wall ran up to a very huge guy and smacked him so hard he still has trouble eating corn on the cob. He fractured his jaw! Then the rest of you came at us swinging. Oh, we fought back and beat you up, sure, but I learned a lesson that night.

"I learned the lesson my dog had. We, and society, had you guys cornered and you came at us. And you had nothing to lose. We threatened you TOO much. You guys felt your lives were at stake and you were going to go down swinging. That's the day I decided to resign from the Mustangs. That's the day I knew somebody was going to get killed if I kept endorsing our philosophy. We pushed the Eagles, and they were pushing back.

"I have to go, Dan, I have a 5:00 a.m. flight out of here tomorrow. Thanks for letting me tell you that story."

I shook his hand, "I think that speech was even better than the one you made earlier. Goodbye."

"Do you have a second to say a prayer together?"

"No, I pray alone."

Chapter 3

The warm spring sunshine felt so nice after the long snowy winter. That Saturday morning found us in the garden putting in our early crops of radish and sweet corn. Mary, Clyde's girlfriend, Bo Schlitz, and I comprised our workforce. Angie Holden was out there too, but her job mainly consisted of walking around and telling us what we were doing wrong.

Mary was an attractive young internal medicine resident at the military hospital at Thompson. Sharing Clyde's love of the outdoors, she loved spending weekends out in the woods. She did have her hands full in the relationship, not with Clyde, but rather with his wisecracking friends.

While I worked a few rows over from her, I said, "Hey Mary, I'm extremely fatigued and feel the need for immediate bed rest. What do you think is wrong with me?"

"I told you, Dan, I'm a physician, not a veterinarian." She was learning fast.

Bo was poking holes in the ground and I was dropping and covering seeds while we worked down the row. I looked up and saw my friend, in only a tee shirt, wiping sweat off his brow.

"Bo, it's only fifty-eight degrees out here. What's the matter with you?"

He huffed, "I don't know. I'm not feeling too well right now. I think I'm coming down with something."

"Then go in and rest a while. I can finish the radishes."

While he walked back toward the bunkhouse, I decided I needed a break. I walked over to Clyde's cabin. He sat on a stump cleaning a rifle. I took a seat on the grass next to him.

Clyde said, "I'm sorry for getting a little out of hand with Greene the other night."

"No problem." Nothing more needed to be said. I recalled from one of Tom Pine's talks about the function of emotions being to prepare the body for action, mostly fight or flight. Emotions put us in a state of readiness. But Clyde's rage had outlived its purpose. He knew it.

We both looked up to see a skein of geese flying north, either calling out directions to each other or just 'chatting'. After Clyde returned to his rifle, I said, "Notice anything wrong with Bo?"

Clyde shrugged his shoulders and said, "No, seems fine to me. I took him to the pharmacy the last time to get his meds refilled; he seemed okay."

"He's sweating a lot. I noticed it the other night. He said he was out jogging."

Clyde snickered and said, "Bo doesn't jog. Angie and I both have been on him about getting out for walks more often. He's getting too heavy."

I looked at Clyde's gun, "What kind of rifle is that?"

"This? This is a conventional rifle that fires rounds. I had one in the Army."

"Don't you use one of those new laser weapons when you hunt?"

"Yeah, sure. Those are more humane. This is a walk-in-the-woods rifle, for self-protection. All true outdoorsmen have one of these. Laser weapons are heavy and need recharging all the time. They may not be ready if a predator is around."

"So, it's not the same rifle you had in the Army?"

"Oh, no. You had to turn in all G.I. firearms when you were discharged."

"You were in a rifle company in the Army, right?"

"Yeah. I only did a year on active duty, since we still had so many men left over from that scare with Mexico. I was stationed at Fort Polk, Louisiana. Things were pretty boring because I mostly stood guard duty. I was only in the field a couple of months."

"Escorting a survey team or something like that?"

"Yes, in the uninhabited area to the northwest of Louisiana. I was told that back in the 22nd century, when the weather started to get bad, the military began to confiscate precious metals from depositories in the North. They stored them in vaults they had in caves out there. Well, the freezing weather got worse, and they found they couldn't haul it all out, so they just blasted the cave entrances and left it buried there. We went up there to retrieve it."

"Did you find it?"

"Oh, we found most of it. A few caves were looted during 'The Chaos' when the population was going nuts. But that was my Army experience. After we returned, I was assigned to a warehouse, then discharged, and then converted over to the reserves."

'Big' Ben Holden, Corky, and Frank Miller came out to the garden to work. I had hoped that our 'foreman' Angie would forget about me. I was wrong.

"Hey Kelley, these radishes aren't gonna plant themselves with you sitting on your big, fat butt up there."

I thumbed my nose at her, but stood up. "Well," I said to Clyde, "I have to go tell Frank I had to sell him in exchange for those Greene passes."

"Good luck."

I walked over to Frank who was taking over my radish planting. "Hi, Frank, old buddy."

He looked up at me, "I don't like the sound of that. What did you get me into this time?"

"Well, I needed to get backstage passes for that Marv Greene thing the other night. I had to get them from Lisa Richardson up at the school. In exchange, I sorta promised her you'd go out with her."

I was expecting the yelling to commence, but Frank simply said, "Lisa Richardson? She was the student body president in high school, right? She's single? Sure, I'll go out with her, she's pretty."

I dodged a bullet with that one, went back to work, and completed my shift about noon. One good thing about having kids was I had to watch them at opportune times. To let my wife come out and do garden work, I had to take a turn, watch the kids, and maybe catch part of the baseball game on television.

When I entered the living room, Annie was trying to teach her little brother how to dance, but he kept losing his balance and falling over.

When she looked at me, she said, "Daddy, ice ceam?"

"No, you pulled that on me before, young lady. No ice cream until after supper."

After I ate lunch and the kids were sacked out, I heard a car go by the cabin and up toward the bunkhouse. I looked out the window, and saw none other than Frank Davis getting out of a

44

cab. He took a suitcase out of the back seat while the driver unloaded two large bags out of the trunk. I opened the door and waved him over.

Frank D. had been my first friend after checking into Delk Hall and the orphanage in seventh grade. We joined the Eagles together. A very smart person, Frank earned a law degree at a young age, became a tax attorney, and moved to Florida to practice. I had last seen him before Annie was born. After a brief courtship, he married last year and stunned us all by not inviting anyone to the wedding. I had not received even an email from him since. My friend approached, and I saw his famous black rimmed glasses and the five o'clock shadow he usually grew by noon.

"Sorry, buddy, there's no soliciting here," I said.

He met me on the steps and we hugged.

"Hey, Dan. How are you doing?"

"Great. I'd invite you in, but I got kids sleeping. Up for a visit?"

"Yeah. Long overdue."

"Coming to the campfire meeting this evening?"

"Sure."

"Put your stuff in the bunkhouse. Clyde finished his log cabin last fall, so there's an empty room. Bo should be up there, maybe sleeping, but you remember where everything is."

"Sure. See you tonight. I'll stop by and get you; I want to see those kids."

Precisely at six o'clock Frank came by. After greeting my family and being unsuccessful in getting Annie to talk to him, we walked to our Saturday night cookout spot back near the entrance to the bunkhouse. All the guys, Angie and Dr. Mary attended. Tom Pine and his wife, Diane, drove down from their house up near the university. Corky cooked steaks on our natural stone grill.

We dispensed with the 'awareness' group format of the meeting, and spent the night in celebration of Frank Davis' visit and catching him up on what went on since he left the area.

Angie, who did pretty good impersonations of all of us, retold the tale of Clyde Hastings, Corky Wall, and Wheeze, a Goth friend of the Eagles retrieving my parents' vehicle from down territory. To cross the Illinois River, they inflated pontoons, lashed them to the sides, and pulled it over with ropes. Well, the rope broke, much to the dismay of Clyde who was riding over on it. When Angie described the scene of Clyde standing up on top, fists raised, cursing at Corky on the shore, everyone was laughing so hard we must have awakened every sleeping animal in the woods.

The vehicle finally was snagged about two miles downstream, but Corky reported that Clyde kept swearing at him for the rest of the trip. Corky's assurance that the Coast Guard in New Orleans would have saved him before he went out into the Gulf of Mexico had done little to cheer Clyde up. Of course Wheeze, who addressed Clyde as Huckleberry Hastings, only made matters worse.

As the stories and laughter continued, probably the most distracted and reserved was our prodigal son, Frank Davis. He responded to questions about his job and wife with generalities instead of specifics. I got the sense that something was rotten in the state of Florida.

I tiptoed through the house the next morning at 5:00 a.m. for fear of waking the babies and my wife. I had left the party around midnight, but was kept awake by those clowns laughing until after one. I grabbed my laser weapon, and walked out into the brisk morning air. I saw Frank Davis up at the campsite, attempting to gather dirty dishes and glasses used during the festivities. I waved him over.

"Frank, I'm going to be a lookout for Clyde while he photographs some birds. Come with me. Wait here, I'll get us some coffees."

The three of us walked silently through the forest to the south until we came upon a large clearing. Frank and I sat on a fallen tree trunk while Clyde walked out to the middle to set up his tripod.

"What time did you get to bed?" I asked Frank in a hushed tone.

"Two. I see you still like the early morning."

"Best time of the day. This way I don't have to act civilized for at least a few hours. So tell me, what went wrong in Florida?"

Frank looked down and said, "Same old Kelley, nothing ever gets by you. What was your first clue?"

"Clues. Oh, the fact you never told us you were coming, you didn't call me to pick you up at the airport, and you pulled enough luggage out of that cab for a visit of at least a year."

"Everything I own is in those bags."

"I also see you didn't bring the wife."

"There's no more wife; there's no more job. I don't know where to start. I had a great job where I was moving up fast. You know, I did the tax returns for both senators from Florida."

"Really? How much did they pay?"

Frank chuckled, "Surprisingly a lot less than I did. You'd be surprised how little taxes really rich people pay. But anyway, I was doing well; I passed the CPA exam within a year. That and my law degree had me on the fast track. Then, I met an amazing girl. The rest is like a blur. We had a quick courtship, eloped, and then settled in at my apartment. Of course, her family blamed me for the elopement.

"They were stinking rich by the way. After 'Daddy' cooled off, he gave up trying to get us divorced and opted for making me more presentable to high society. He was a big time trial attorney and wanted me to join his firm, convert to being a trial attorney, and take over for him in his elderly years. I refused of course, that being the very reason I left here. That's when things started to go south.

"My wife's luncheons with friends at her father's country club went from one day a week to four, from two hours each to five."

"Was she drinking?"

"Like a fish. Of course, 'Dad' blamed me for making his daughter a lush, even though she confided in me she was stealing from her parent's liquor cabinet when she was eight. One night I came home to find the apartment cleaned out, along with our bank account. We got divorced, and that turned into an annulment. It seemed as if 'Daddy' knew the judge."

"Was she Catholic?"

"Yeah. Why?"

"If approved it allows them to remarry in the church. 'Daddy' probably also knew a priest."

"Then, I got fired from my job; it seemed that 'Daddy' also knew my managing partner. I had to get a job with a cut-rate tax service to pay my rent and save up enough to buy a plane ticket. I slept in a sleeping bag for two months."

"You could have called us, Frank."

"I was ashamed and embarrassed."

"I'm your 'brother'! I slept on the cot next to yours since the seventh grade. I ought to box your ears in right now."

"Guilty, your honor." He raised his palm as if swearing an oath, and smiled wanly, with his head hung down.

"What are you going to do now?"

"I'm going to go see my sister this afternoon, then Hightower tomorrow, and see if I can get my old investigator job back until I can figure something out."

"Okay, then. You're back home now. Rely on your family. But tell me, how did you like living in the big city?"

"I thought it would be different. I thought it would be exciting. I hated it. The traffic was awful. People honked and gave the finger to each other. There were fistfights at four way stops. Imagine that! Two drivers would avoid yielding for four seconds to get out for a five minute fistfight. One night, coming back from my wife's parents, a homeless guy climbed on our hood and urinated on our windshield."

"You did slip him a token for cleaning your windshield, didn't you?"

Frank chuckled, "Turns out it's a very efficient method; I'm thinking of taking out a patent."

Just then my handcomp buzzed wildly. I pulled up a message that read "Ben - Compound" with a red flashing light under it. Clyde, who was looking at his simultaneously, quickly grabbed his tripod and started running toward us.

"Trouble?" Frank asked.

"Signal Red. Myers set up this emergency call system several years ago when we had some trespassers. When one of us gets in a jam, he dials red and the rest come to his aid. We hooked up the wives also."

After Clyde caught up with us, we all ran toward Ben's cabin. We approached seeing Ben and most of the guys standing near his back deck. I saw Angie and Marie standing by my cabin, looking down at us.

While we caught our breath, Ben said, "Seems we lost Schlitz. Who saw him last?"

I looked at Frank Davis who said, "No, he wasn't there yesterday when I got here, and wasn't there when I went to bed or got up."

"I saw him yesterday morning in the garden. He was sweaty; said he didn't feel well. I told him to go lay down," I added.

"Think he overdosed?"

"Corky is checking his room now," Ben said.

Just then Corky Wall came running toward us.

"OD?"

"Maybe worse," Corky said while he held up all three of Bo's medicine bottles. All three were full to the top.

"Clyde," Ben went on, "when did you take him to get these filled?"

"Gee, I know there was still snow on the ground. Early March I think."

Ben said, "He quit taking his meds. Crap! Okay, let's fan out. I remember he was fond of the campgrounds we stayed at that one winter when we ran away from detention. You know, with the caves? Clyde, why don't you and Kelley check there? Corky, check the barn, machine shed, and near the garden. Davis, get Angie and go through his room. Miller, check all around the horseshoe ridge and east of there. I'll call the city police and get Tom Pine down here. Let's hit it, guys."

Clyde and I turned and headed toward his cabin while Ben yelled to us, "Clyde, don't go in that cave without a gun."

50

"It'll take us two hours to walk out there," Clyde said, "Let's take my Omnitraker."

We were soon flying down the trail out to the caves. I mean flying because Clyde was going so fast, when we hit a high spot the all-terrain vehicle would actually fly into the air. He was wearing his 'Old World'-style side arm and I clung to a laser weapon in one hand and held on with the other.

At the cave entrance, Clyde held his pistol in one hand and a flashlight in the other. He told me, "I'll be alright. Take a walk around the hill and check back there."

I returned before Clyde came out of the cave. Although it was only about ten minutes, it seemed like an hour before he came out. "See anything?" I shook my head. "Okay, let's go straight east from here and check out that trail that runs along our property line. Then we can…"

A ring from Clyde's handcomp interrupted him. When he answered, a voice said, "Clyde, we found him. You know that tall pine tree, southeast of Kelley's cabin? Bo climbed up it. Is Kelley with you?"

"Yeah."

"Okay, bring him. He will only talk to Kelley. Get here as fast as possible."

"Okay. Any idea what he's doing up there?"

"He hasn't specified, but it looks like to me he's going to jump off."

I didn't think Clyde could drive that Omnitraker one mile per hour faster without killing both of us. However, I could only picture Bo taking a swan dive off that tree. Why the heck didn't I just take him to the hospital the moment I saw him sweating? What the heck was wrong with me? I was so darn self-absorbed and moody about my own stupid little problems that I couldn't even see a 'brother' in need! What if one of my kids had something wrong and I didn't see it? When would I wake up? When I'm a pallbearer at Bo's funeral?

We rode up to the spot. Tom Pine had joined the group also, and all were looking up.

"Says he'll only talk to you, Dan," Ben said.

"Well, I have to take Pine. Come on, Tom, I don't know what to say. You've had all the psych training."

Tom responded, "He doesn't need an analyst; he needs a friend. Go be that."

I was shaking so hard I didn't know how I walked to the base of the tree. I looked up and could see him. I bit my lip hard and repeated to myself: Bo is not dying today.

The tree trunk was not thick and had spindly, long branches, and only sparse pine needles. I could see Bo clearly, but he was really high up there. He stood on a branch, and held on to the trunk, with shirt and shoes off.

"Bo," I yelled up, "what are you doing up a tree, buddy?"

He laughed hysterically, and then said, "I climb the pine and walk the line, Dan. I can see Russia from up here and soldiers from all the battles and the star that guided the three kings to the Christ child."

He was certainly talking gibberish.

"I want you to come down out of the tree now, Bo. Please."

"Can't think down there, can't think. Pressure's too high. Lower barometric pressure is the key, Dan, just ask Al Myers. My head hurts down there."

"Let's talk about it, only down here."

"The line runs both ways, Dan. Things don't line up in a perfect universe, only an imperfect one. Mine eyes have seen the glory of the coming of the American Nurses Association, and the kiln, and the anniversary."

"Do you want me to come up there, Bo?" I didn't want to. I would have done anything to save my friend, only climbing up that tree wasn't high on the list.

"I'm not sure this branch will hold both of us." He started jumping up and down and I was terrified when I saw it bow under him.

"Bo, don't jump on the branch!"

"Okay. Kind of creepy anyway. I don't have faith in nature anymore and home is where the heart is and I never could understand Picasso paintings anyway. No angles, no lines. Just what does that say about me?"

"I don't know, what you're saying isn't making sense to me."

"Not making any sense to you? You should hear what I'm saying from inside my head! I sure could use some ice cream, Dan; think the ice cream shop will deliver up here?" He then laughed.

"Let's go get some. Come on, Bo. Come down here and we'll go for ice cream."

"Just us?"

"I promise. Nobody else."

"Okay."

Much to my surprise, and I'm sure to the others waiting some distance away, Bo started to climb down from the tree. I didn't understand most of what he had said, but got the impression that suicide was not a reason he went up there. He immediately greeted me with a sweaty bear hug. The perspiration had soaked through his pants.

"I think I'm in dire need to go to the hospital, Dan."

"Okay, I'll take you. Just us. We'll stop for ice cream on the way."

We turned and walked, arm in arm. He wouldn't let go. After we got to my truck, I noticed one of my fast thinking friends had put a blanket and a small sack containing Bo's medication bottles on the seat. When I drove out of the compound, I saw a fire truck and an ambulance parked near my cabin. I could just picture all those firemen running out to the tree with a net.

Bo sat in the passenger seat, wrapped in the blanket and asked, "You don't think Annie saw me, do you, Dan?"

"I don't think so."

"She's a sweetheart. Little kids are great; they don't care if you make sense all the time, they just want to hear a story. Grownups bother me. Look at Al Myers. He's too stiff. He thinks A plus B is always C. But A and B sometimes vary, change, they are not what they appear. So when A plus B doesn't equal C, it drives him nuts. He can't handle it. Up in the pine tree, math rules fade away. Ever wonder about these things, Dan?"

"More than you know."

Going through the drive-up at the ice cream shop, I got Bo a cup of chocolate and we continued on to the hospital on the Thompson Defense Base. After finishing his treat, he said, "Thanks for the ice cream, Dad."

At first I thought he had just mispronounced my name, but then got the impression that Bo was riding with the dad he never had. When I thought back at how early treatment could have helped him, I cursed our system. This was a prime example of how Centura dealt with its orphans. Heck, just give them an old army blanket and a bunk to sleep in. They're just

going to grow up and scoop cow 'poop' out of a barn. There's
no need to put those kids in special classes or provide them
with mental healthcare. It's a waste of resources. We need to
save all that stuff for the chemistry majors.

I sat in the waiting room of the psychiatry intake for over
two hours. I had already called back to inform everyone that we
had made it here. Finally a young female psychiatry resident
came in the room. "Did you come in with Beauregard Schlitz?"

"Yeah."

"Are you family?"

"He has no living relatives; I'm the closest thing he's got."

"Do you have those pill bottles?"

I showed them to her.

"Okay, over a month would you say?"

"Yeah."

"Let's sit down."

We took seats in the empty room.

"I've admitted him. I'm just on call for the weekend; his
regular doctor will see him tomorrow. I'm only assuming, but I
think he'll be here for a while. You can call his doctor
tomorrow. Are you Mr. Kelley?"

"Yeah."

"Good job out at the pine tree by the way."

"Thanks. Is he really bad?"

"He's ill. There's a strong likelihood he may recover quickly,
but we're a few days away from making that determination.
You know him well, correct?"

"Sure. We're like brothers."

"Can you help me with something I picked up?"

"I'll try."

"He's never had a repeat admission since the initial hospitalization. He's never missed an outpatient appointment, never let his prescriptions lapse, and other than being overweight he's been the model patient. Any reason you know why he quit taking his meds?"

"Not really. Do you think he was suicidal?"

"I never got that indication. The whole thing just strikes me as odd."

"How so?"

"It's just that I got the impression he quit taking his meds on purpose, that he had a purpose. What that purpose was I couldn't elicit from him. Any ideas?"

"Not really. He was turned down for his nursing license a while back. Other than that, no."

"Oh well, his regular doc may get into that with him. Okay then, you might as well go home. He'll probably be sleeping for a day or two."

"Do you mind if I stay with him?"

"He's probably not going to know you're there."

"That's not important. I think it's more for my mental health than his."

I stayed next to Bo's bed the rest of that day, all night, and into the next morning. About 7:00 a.m. he sat up, looked at me with a blank expression, turned around, and went back to sleep.

Since I had to get to work, I left. In the parking lot, I ran into Tom Pine and Corky Wall who were just arriving. They made such an odd pair crossing the parking lot. Tom was a tall, robust man with sandy gray hair, and looked older than his thirty plus years. Corky was short and stocky, a toned body and powerful biceps complimented his much younger look.

I filled them in on what Bo had told me and what the doctor had said. I finished with, "I should have seen ..."

Tom held up a hand to stop me. "I don't want to hear it. I just got all over this guy," motioning toward Corky, "on the way up here. Bo is twenty-seven, we can't be babysitters. You missed it, I missed it, and everybody missed it. He's never done this before and he caught us off guard. He's overweight and sweats a lot. Best evidence has it that Bo stopped taking the meds on his own; so unless we want to set up our own medicine-dispensing psych ward in the bunkhouse, I suggest we cancel the guilt trips. Thanks an order, Dan."

I saluted Tom in jest, "Aye, aye, sir."

Chapter 4

Bo remained in the hospital while the rest of us tried to carry on with our lives. I had visited him on the Tuesday after he was admitted. He was ambulatory, but shuffled around the ward, drooling, with that blank stare on his face. I felt bad for him. Was this going to be a lifelong thing? The treatment seemed just as bad as when his symptoms flared up. The look on his face gave me the impression that his thoughts were taken away, that his personhood was reduced to a numb blob shuffling through reality.

Thursday noon found me grabbing a bite at a trendy eatery on the Northside. I had compromised with the veggo-fascists and had a salad. While I was going over my notes for my meeting with Mr. Greene, I looked up to see a familiar face coming toward me.

"Dan, I got this food to go but I'll eat it here. I need to talk to you; may I join you?" She then sat down without an invitation.

Elizabeth Barney was a freelance menace and regionally-renowned pain in the neck. She had hated me since elementary school.

"Betsy, I didn't know you ate lunch with bohemians."

"I have to serve my constituents whether I like them or not. You do know I'm on the city council now?"

"I've heard it about fifty times, yes."

"So how are the 'backwoods boys'? Still practicing human sacrifices down there around the fire?"

"Every week. You should join us someday."

She ignored that and asked, "But speaking of constituents, you aren't one, are you? Because you don't pay any city property taxes, do you?"

"I think the fact that we don't live in the city could be a reason. We pay taxes. We pay sales tax for the things we sell here."

"But not for the goods you sell at the military base. This is why I'm going to propose a bill to annex your property."

"We own four square miles, mostly undeveloped. Does the city want all that?"

"No, only the part with your dwellings."

"City annexation means city services. How long will our taxes take to pay for the four mile sewer line you're going to have to run out there? How about trash collection? Are you going to run a snowplow out there several times a week?"

"We already have to plow that stupid road we put in for you, out to the end of Frazer's property." She paused and frowned, looking me up and down.

"Oh, nice uniform by the way, are you up here to fix somebody's refrigerator?"

"What is it with you, Betsy? How come you hated me from the day we met?"

"I didn't hate you. Do you mean back in the seventh grade? You never even talked to me. You would just sit there with that dumb look on your face. You were the one who ignored me."

"You can't see past the back of your hand, can you, Betsy? Do you ever think about what was going on with someone else? You took developmental psychology in college, I'm sure.

60

Do you know how intimidating it is for a twelve-year-old boy to talk with a girl who looked as good as you did?"

Betsy wiped off her mouth, stood up, then walked out of the restaurant.

I was stunned. I had not intended to make her angry, but I sure must have found the right button to push.

Mr. Greene's house was even more impressive on the inside. The butler showed me to his study where I noticed the terrazzo floor in the hallway. I had only seen them in history books.

After we were introduced, I shook hands with a very distinguished older gentleman. He was very tall with gray hair at the temples and seemed to possess his son's charisma, only without the ego.

He said, "Please call me Art."

We sat on overstuffed chairs that faced one another.

"Very nice place you have here, Art." I said.

"Thank you, I've been very fortunate. Marvin tells me you're here about your parents and I'm certainly willing to help you. I was looking through my notes earlier and didn't see a Patrick Kelley listed anywhere."

"Oh, his name was O'Dea. Kelley was the name given to me by the orphanage."

"Patrick O'Dea ... hmm, that doesn't ring a bell either. Was he a Leap Frog employee? What did he do?"

"He was sort of a fix-it man, general laborer. I know he took care of the company's beef cattle."

"That might be the problem. I only worked with the site director. Let me give you some history. Leap Frog Technologies was a private corporation not affiliated with the Federal Government. About 3047, they were granted military contracts to recover certain items left during the mini-ice age in the area west and north of Old St. Louis. They erected buildings, outfitted excursions into the countryside, and provided for the general needs of the employees."

"Did they fulfill the contracts?"

"Many of them. I was not privy to what all of them were, but the ones I do know about are classified and I cannot discuss them."

"Can you tell of their general nature?"

"It was mostly equipment used in coding communications or directing troop movements. Equipment that was probably rusted and deteriorated but would be better off not in the hands of the general public. Stuff that was too massive to be flown out."

"No atom bombs?"

Mr. Greene chuckled, "No, nothing as exciting as that. They found equipment in many places throughout the area there. I think the Offutt Air Force Base site in Nebraska was about the furthest away."

"NORAD?"

"No, that place was secured before the military left."

We paused while the butler brought in a tray of coffee and continued after he left.

"Why were you there, sir?"

"Well, about 3053, Leap Frog's workers' compensation insurance carrier began to get a large number of work related injury claims out of that place. They hinted of hazardous working conditions. The insurer complained to OSHA, who complained to the military, who, because of the sensitive nature of the contracts, sent me to investigate the conditions there. I was with the Army Corps of Engineers. I was there, off and on, from June of '53 until New Year's Eve of 3055. The place was wrapping up and expected to close the summer of the next year, but the flood of April 3056 brought things to an early end."

"What was the place like when you got there?"

"A mess. Don't get me wrong, Bernie Kline, Leap Frog site director, ran a tight ship. None of the contracts were compromised. However, the place was attracting all sorts of odd folks. I indicated earlier that this was a civilian enterprise. The military did not supply police order; Kline had his own rent-a-cops. People came to work on the labor gangs, people with shady pasts. There were also prostitutes. I did manage to get the workplace problems fixed up, but there were some real nut jobs around there.

"And the pirates I heard about?"

"Yeah. Those clowns had their own thing going. They went around digging up bank vaults trying to find treasures. All they got were rotted bundles of useless U.S. currency because the government had done away with paper money years before. I guess they got a few coin collections out of safe deposit boxes. Most of the pirates, however, were arrested and prosecuted."

"So what does all this mean for someone like my father?"

"I only worked with Kline. He had a deputy, Leo Gustav, who worked gathering the labor gangs for projects. Actually Gustav had a guy, Bob Wilson, who arranged most of that stuff. Keep in mind, those laborers were freelance, not Leap Frog employees. Wilson would have known your dad if anyone had. Of course, he either drowned in the flood or died of old age. He was old then. Gustav's dead too. He died during an excursion north the last year I was there. We know Kline died in the flood because they found his body."

"How did men and material get there?"

"They had a private airstrip, however, most got there by riverboat."

"From where?"

"Vicksburg."

"So, you were stationed there for those two years?"

"My official duty station was Fort Polk, that's where my family was. I flew back and forth for trips home every now and then."

"So what are your assumptions about my father? Any hints?"

Mr. Greene got a serious look on his face and said, "Dan, I just want you to know that if your dad wandered into the settlement and was in the general labor force, he may have been involved in some of the illegal shenanigans going on there. Marvin told me most of the story. Your whole family was there?"

"Yeah. I was born there. But all my records went south with the water."

"And when did he leave Old St. Louis?"

"July or August of '55."

"And you wound up where?"

"About one hundred miles due south of Centura."

"That's odd. That's not even in the area the pirates usually visited. Was he headed here?"

"I don't know. Any suggestions?"

"Well, you could check the Leap Frog records. A lot of them were used in a lawsuit by relatives of flood victims. I heard litigation is still going on in that case. About a thousand people drowned in that flood. Now, did I hear correctly, that you were picked up by a Marine helicopter out of Thompson?"

"Correct."

"Who called it in?"

"I assumed my Dad did. He had a small radio in his vehicle."

"I would suggest you follow up on that. You might get some clues."

"Thank you, that's all I had."

"Anything else I can help you with?"

We stood and I shook his hand.

"I guess that's it. Wow, you sure have done well for yourself, Art. How did you end up in this lovely town?"

"After I left Leap Frog I was assigned a few more inspection projects, and then transferred here in '57 to work at the base. I resigned my commission soon afterward because I got the opportunity of a lifetime. I got in on the ground floor of a natural gas exploration outfit in Guatemala and we struck it rich. But it didn't end well."

"How so?"

"My wife died soon afterward, and then I lost control of my son with that gang and the drugs and alcohol. He has talked to me at length about that, Dan, and his involvement with you. He is truly sorry for the problems he caused you."

"Yeah. We've talked and I think he feels that way. Thank you again, sir."

"Please let me know how this turns out."

"I will."

I drove home with thoughts running wild. I believed I had made an important ally with Art Greene and would use him in the future to check out leads. However, I still had to talk to someone who knew Patrick O'Dea.

Early Friday afternoon found Corky Wall and I in the machine shed addition, our new headquarters for the genealogy committee. With Frank Davis moving back 'home', we didn't want to disturb him in the bunkhouse. We had our camping gear with us since we were going on an overnight. Ben Holden was late. After we heard a car approach, we saw Clyde Hastings enter through an opening in the large sliding doors of the shed.

"Well, Greene checks out," he said.

Corky asked, "How'd you get that?"

"I went up to the reserve center on the base. We have access to the Defense Department personnel database on our quantacomps up there." The virtual personal assistant spoke from his handcomp, "Arthur Wallace Greene, Georgia Tech ROTC grad, received an officer's commission and spent two years in New Orleans studying the river and delta systems. He was even a contributing author of a published journal article on the subject. Transferred to Fort Polk, Louisiana and was assigned to TDY, that's temporary duty, at several localities throughout the region to inspect structures. He worked mostly as a building inspector. Between June '53 and December '55, he was assigned to the Leap Frog site at Old St. Louis. He was noted for being extremely helpful in assisting personnel to correct deficiencies there. After Fort Polk, he was transferred to Thompson Defense Base, Centura, Illinois Territory in April 3057. There he resigned his commission, with honors, on December 31 of that same year. An impressive record."

Corky said, "I got my information from general quantanet sources. They indicate Mr. Greene was a minority partner in the Estuary Hydrofracturing Company of Cobán, Guatemala. He was an extraction design manager. He worked at that from January '58 until about five years later, when a large oil company from Venezuela bought out the company. I read they made millions on the deal."

"Anything else, Clyde?" I asked.

"One Bernard Kline, no military record.

Corky said, "Bernard Kline, several ladder positions with Leap Frog Technologies, then Site Director, Old St. Louis site. No wife or kids. He died from drowning, April 7, 3056.

Clyde continued, "Mr. Leo Gustav, entered the Marines, went to boot camp and then infantry school, then discharged two months later."

"Discharged how?"

"Conscientious objector."

Corky went on, "Leo Gustav, several positions at Leap Frog, then Deputy Site Director for Operations, Old St. Louis. Not much on him. He went missing sometime in late 3055.Whereabouts unknown."

Clyde reported that there wasn't any record for a Bob Wilson, and Corky indicated he wasn't listed on the Leap Frog employee roster.

"Thanks guys," I said, "but this is enough of this madness. To the woods, Cork."

"Hey Clyde," Corky said, "Dan, Ben and I are going on an overnight, want to go?"

"No. Mary is coming down and we're going to watch a couple of movies."

Clyde never spoke much about his love life and resisted questions on the subject. But that didn't stop us. I asked, "Gonna smooch on the couch, Clyde, do some 'canoodling'?"

"Shut up."

Corky asked, "Is she a good kisser, Clyde? How would you rate her, on a scale of one to ten?"

"None of your business."

"Does she have a pet name for you? What is it? 'Huggy Bear'?"

Clyde walked toward the door, "The crap I take from you two. I'm going to start looking for some new friends." He passed Ben as he was walking in.

"Ready?" Ben asked.

We started off on foot toward the caves. We couldn't have had a better day. The forest, waking up from winter, had a bright green color from new leaves on the trees. Blossoms were flying everywhere in the modest breeze. Spongy to the step, the forest carpet still contained water from the thaw. We felt our worries fly away while we walked, silently, soaking it all in. The two plus mile walk out to the winter caves seemed to take no time at all because we soon approached the rocky hills.

The Eagles were out here, almost a decade ago, escaping an unfortunate situation back in Centura. We spent an entire winter in these caves, reexamining and rededicating our lives. The woods and the prairie didn't cause a sudden spiritual awakening; it was gradual. Thought patterns changed out here. A good dose of nature swept away obstacles. We became less envious and more thankful. Not harming us at all, I realized that the time off from school years ago was a benefit and not a waste of time. We took our lessons from the 'school of hard knocks'.

We entered the winter cave and, after checking all spaces for 'critters', built a fire with wood stored from last fall. After unloading our cooking utensils and mess kits, we headed down to the lake to fish.

Since fish in the uninhabited areas had few predators, we soon pulled walleye out of that lake like nobody's business. Our jokes and laughter continued through cleaning and cooking. I fried up some hash browns while Corky heated up some of his famous spicy lemon butter sauce for the fish. After having worked for dinner, Corky and I had two platefuls while big Ben had three. We made Ben do the dishes.

While Corky scaled the hill next to our cave to get a better signal for his handcomp to call back to the settlement, Ben and I chatted. "Did I tell you I ran into Betsy Barney this week?" I asked Ben.

"Really? What was on her mind?"

"She reminded me of her annexation proposal."

"It's not a big deal. Our property is within a federal jurisdiction and we pay taxes on it now. Annexation would only transfer that money over to the city. It's about the same amount. Why I have Ms. Hightower keeping an eye on it, is so we get the additional services. You know, all the extra money around here goes to Northside projects. North Shore Drive got resurfaced last year and South Shore Drive is full of potholes. Barney is just like the rest of that pro-Northside core on the council; it's not political, it's personal."

"Do you think it will pass?"

"The council is split even right now, that means the president of the council gets to vote, and she lives on North Shore Drive. Need I say more? How did your encounter end?"

"The same as ever. Betsy got mad at me and stormed out."

"Dan, maybe you should do a little separation between the political and the personal also. I have to go before that council, and we need to communicate how we can provide a benefit to this community. They are the political entity we have to deal with. There is no other. Unless our rights are violated, Hightower can't do a thing."

Corky took the first watch from 11:00 p.m. until 1:00 a.m.; Ben took the second until three. Only Ben didn't have to wake me for mine because Corky's snoring had already taken care of that. I replenished the fire and sat near the cave entrance with the laser weapon. The forest was calm and quiet.

Perhaps Ben had been right. During that run in with Betsy, I had let those old feelings surface. Poor, old orphan Dan. The name-calling and the mudslinging and the fistfight days were over. We had won; we were exonerated. Now the playing field was even, and I had to play by the same rules as everyone else. I couldn't shake the feeling, however, that there were leftover hard feelings. Something in me wasn't settled.

Chapter 5

"Hello, may I speak to Ms. Lisa Richardson, please?"

"You know it's me, you bonehead."

"Oh, I thought the maid had answered."

"Right. Since I moved home, my parents are making me do the cleaning and laundry. So, I'm the darn maid around here. What's up, Dan?"

"I need to talk to your dad. Think that would be possible?"

"Why don't you call his office?"

"I hate going there, it's too formal."

"Okay, how about tomorrow afternoon, about two?"

"On a Sunday? Are you sure?"

"Sure."

"Okay, see you then. Bye."

"Hey! Not so fast. You have to bring Frank Miller. Sorry, that's the deal."

"Okay, bye."

At first, I was surprised by Frank Miller's attitude toward Lisa, but on the drive up to the base on Sunday, I got the impression that he actually liked her. We approached the house on the senior officer's row and it was quite impressive. Even though I now had a much better truck than in high school, I remembered to park in the back.

Mrs. Richardson allowed us entry. She looked a lot like Lisa, tall and slender. When I had first met Captain Richardson, the

Naval commander at the base, they were separated, but they were obviously back together now.

"Oh, Daniel Kelley, I've heard a lot about you from both my husband and daughter. He seems rather fond of you. Tell me, how did you crack the exterior of that old walnut?"

"I had to promise him I would join the Navy."

Frank said, "What impressed me about him was his taste in women."

I just looked at Frank and thought "Really!" Boy, was I going to rub his nose in it later, for sure. Mrs. Richardson just ate it up. She beamed.

"You, young man, are going to marry my daughter. Next weekend, clear your calendar."

Lisa then walked down the hall toward us. She grabbed Frank's hand, "We'll be on the back porch. Dan, Dad's on the phone, wait in the hall outside his study until he calls you."

I sat across the hall from the double sliding doors. Sometimes I forgot just how important Captain Richardson was. People in this town respected the Army, Navy, and Air Force commanders at Thompson. They were like Civil War generals on a battlefield. Their power was almost absolute. They controlled the police force, fire department, power plant, and all medical care for the community.

Since the nation converted to universal health care and the city couldn't staff a city medical center, the base had the only hospital in town. The Defense Department also spent a ton of money to reimburse schools and other businesses for services they provided to the military, and the commanders decided how those funds would be spent. They even outranked the mayor of Centura. People knew that life here could be a living hell if one of them got ticked off at you.

"Kelley. Enter," I heard from inside. The captain sat at his desk in full dress whites, even on a Sunday.

"Greetings, Commodore," I said. He smiled at me because I was one of the few who called him by his brevet rank. A commodore held the official rank of captain in the Navy, and was an officer with command of more than one ship. It was an outdated term, not officially used since the Civil War, but he still got a kick out of it.

"Did you hear I'm retiring soon?" he said.

"Really? Are you going to move down South?"

"Actually, we bought one of those high-end log homes in that neighborhood just east of you guys. We'll be neighbors."

"Oh, my. I guess we'll have to tone down all those drunken orgies we have down there."

"Oh, no. In fact, I had better be invited to some. Please, have a seat." We shook hands heartily. "Hey, Dan, are you working on getting Lisa married off? She moved back home, you know."

"I heard. We're working on it, sir."

"So, does this writer friend of yours like her?"

"I think he does. He just gave your wife the sappiest compliment I ever heard."

"Well, that's good. Keep supporting that, okay? So, what can I do for you today?"

"Can you look at this?" I handed him a copy of the log from the helicopter that picked me up on the prairie years ago.

After donning his reading glasses, he read it. "Hmm. This is a helicopter search and rescue log. From 3055?" At the end, he looked up at me, "Where did you get this?"

"From my brother, years ago. When he was up here searching records about my parents."

"How did he get it?"

"From the records office here on the base. Freedom of Information Act request, I imagine.

"Okay, then. I'll tell you what, Dan, there are all kinds of codes on here. I don't know what the heck they mean. I have people read these to me. I'll give this to Mrs. Henderson over in intelligence and have her find out for you. I'll have her call you. Give her a week or two."

"Thank you, sir."

"So, what are you going to do now that you're graduating from college?"

"I'm not sure yet. Graduate school, maybe."

"Ever think about a Navy commission? I could make that happen."

"Really?"

"I'm the commander and yes, I can."

"I have a wife and two babies. I would hate to be apart right now."

"It would only be a few months training. Then you could be back here working in Mrs. Henderson's office. You could be home every night and on weekends."

"Guess I'd have to think about it."

"Okay, then, anything else?"

"No, sir." I stood up and saluted him.

"Hey, the Navy doesn't salute inside. I'd make you drop and give me twenty, Kelley, but it's Sunday. And that's grunt and jarhead stuff." He cracked a crooked smile.

I assaulted Frank on the way home, "'I admire him for his taste in women.' Really, Frank?"

He turned toward the side window and blushed a little.

74

"Please excuse me while I pull over to the side of the road and puke about eight times," I added.

"Hey, I've heard you kissing up to Marie's mom. You married guys don't have a corner on the market, you know."

I decided to let Frank off the hook, primarily because I was glad he and Lisa were getting along so well.

I commented, "He said he was going to give that message to intelligence for them to look at."

"I'm surprised we didn't think of that before now. So, Mr. Greene suggested that?"

"Yeah. I just assumed Patrick called, and the Marines came running."

"That's why we have to go back over everything periodically," Frank went on. "We may have made a simple assumption about something, an assumption so obvious but nonetheless incorrect."

"Do you think we've made others?"

Frank looked at me. "Nothing that comes to mind right now. But I am getting that strange old feeling again."

"What feeling?"

"The one Tom Pine had eight years ago and is having again right now. We talked about this at the campfire meeting last night, after you left. Nothing specific, it's more of a general feeling. We find it strange that everyone we know who actually talked to Patrick O'Dea is either dead or presumed dead, with the exception of you and your brother. Do you remember anything about your mom?"

"That's the weird part. I remember riding in the back of that vehicle, and it was bumpy. I recall my Dad in the pilot seat, looking over at mom every now and then. I remember a lady sitting shotgun; I could see the back of her head. But I can't picture her face. I can't even remember her ever talking to me."

"Pine suggested hypnosis. Would you be willing to submit to that?"

"I would be willing to do anything."

The next day I noticed the waiting room at the university sleep lab had a poster on the wall that read, "Falling Asleep in this Classroom is a Requirement."

Tom Pine and another gentleman then entered to greet me.

"Dan, this is Dr. Weston," Tom said.

I shook hands with him.

"He has agreed to help us. He is from the psychology department, but we're meeting here because of the soundproof walls. Follow us."

We walked down a hallway and entered a very pleasant room with a couch and two chairs. I took the couch.

Dr. Weston, a very distinguished-looking middle-aged man spoke. "Dan, I don't usually do these things outside of the research arena, especially since you are not a random subject. But I am working on some new techniques and, well, Dr. Pine is very convincing. So, have you ever been hypnotized before?"

"No. I didn't mean any offense with insisting that Tom be here, it's just that I trust him. I don't think he would let you give me a hypnotic suggestion to put a lampshade over my head, or something."

Dr. Weston laughed, "No, I don't do that. No problem. So, you may know, this is all about relaxing. Now, I want you to do some counting for me. I want you to count, in ascending order, all the prime numbers up to one hundred thousand."

"What?" I looked at them strangely until they both started to laugh.

Dr. Weston said pointing to Tom, "Hey, he put me up to it. Okay, seriously, I want you to put your hands on your thighs and fixate on one spot on the back of your right hand."

"Do you want me to lie down?"

"No, stay seated. I hear you have a little girl. Annie, right?"

"Yeah."

"Do you remember holding her for the first time?"

"Yes."

"Okay, no need to answer me anymore. Just think about that little sweetie. Okay, close your eyes now. Think about that little girl. Dan, we're going to talk about some times in your life. Only we're going to talk about more recent times first and then work backwards. Now I just want you to keep concentrating on that hand, think about Annie, and relax." After several moments he spoke again. "Think about your wedding now. Now close your eyes. Okay, Dan, I want you to respond now. What is it like being with the Eagles?"

"Oh, great. They're my brothers; they saved my life."

"Great bunch of guys, I hear. Do you remember things at Delk Hall?"

"Yeah. Bad times."

"How are they bad? How do you feel?"

"Scared. Afraid I'll get hit in the face."

"Now tell me about before Delk Hall, at the little kids' orphanage."

"Great. Pillow fights. Ice cream."

"Dan, you recall the helicopter ride up here, correct?"

"Bouncy. Guys with masks on."

"You were once riding in a vehicle, out on the prairie, correct? Then you got stuck. What did your parents talk about right when that happened?"

"Dad said, "Get the book.""

"What book was that?"

"Don't remember."

"What happened then?"

"They got out, left. I have to pee, so I got out, too."

"Your brother took you out?"

"No brother. It's snowing. I slide down and then see nothing but snow. I heard the helicopter and felt the wind it makes."

"Do you remember riding out on the prairie before getting stuck? I mean even days before that."

"Riding, yes."

"What could you see there from your seat?"

"Mom and Dad."

"What parts of your mom and dad?"

"Dad's head."

"What about the back of mom's head?"

"Can't see it."

"Did you and your brother ever get rowdy in the back? Did your mom ever turn around and scold you?"

"Not ever."

"Okay, Dan, now I want you to pretend something. I want you to pretend that you wanted to get your mom's attention. Imagine crawling up between the front seats and asking her something. Tell me what her face looked like."

"I can't see her face."

"Do you remember being in Old St. Louis?"

"No."

"Can you tell me what your parents talked about, just before you all left there?

"No."

"Do you recall anything your mother said to you?"

"No."

"How about your dad?"

"Not to me, no. He talked to mom."

"Do you remember what he said to her?"

"Get the book."

"Okay, Dan, now let's return to Annie. I want you to take a minute and just think about her again. Then in a minute we'll talk again."

I opened my eyes and looked at the two professors. "Sorry, Dr. Weston. I guess I'm not a good subject."

"No, you were fine," Dr. Weston said.

"But I remember everything, so I couldn't have been hypnotized."

"Oh, you were 'under'," Tom said. "Most people remember everything."

After I thanked Dr. Weston, I walked Tom back to his office.

He said, "Dan, was your mom mute? Did she ever sign?"

"Tom, I wish I could tell you. I'm beginning to wonder if I ever had a mom."

"I think you did. You can't picture her but you mentioned her being at the scene. How 'they got out, left'. Some woman was in that cab with you. If you recall, that doctor who examined you upon arriving in Centura said that you may have had some sort of memory loss due to exposure. We know when the 'copter picked you up, but we don't know when you left the vehicle. It could have been several hours." Tom patted me on the back, "Well, looks like we have to come up with something else to try."

We turned goat milking into a family affair. Early the next morning found my whole family in our barn. Since we rotated duties for Anchor Farms, all of us who lived in the compound pitched in. However, Marie and I were the only two doing the milking that morning. Little Patrick was attempting, unsuccessfully, to catch one of the barn cats and Annie, who watched us for about thirty seconds, was soon off to help her brother. After giving the milk to Corky for processing, we all walked back to the cabin for breakfast.

My jobsite for that day was the log home development just east of our property. I was wiring a new home and couldn't have been happier. The building was closed in, and it was such a pleasure to wire it before the interior walls were installed. Also, Ron had hired two work-study students from the electrical science program at the university, and one was assigned to help me. She was hard working and loved diving in to learn the more advanced stuff. In the late afternoon, I asked her to finish cutting some conduit while I took off early for a personal project.

The first thing I noticed when I entered the humanities building at the college was the missing UXU amphibious vehicle. This was the military half troop carrier/half boat my father used on my family's trek across the prairie, found on the Eagles' mission of discovery eight years earlier. We found it right where it broke down on the day my parents disappeared. Later, another mission was made by my friends to retrieve it. Wheeze, our mechanic friend, restored it and tried unsuccessfully to sell the thing. He found no buyers, so he donated it to the history department and they displayed it in their lobby. They had now taken it out to make room for Dr. Principi's Paleo-Indian exhibit.

I entered the suite of the history department, and was greeted by professors just leaving for the day. Dr. Principi was standing next to a quantacomp console.

I said, "Thank you doctor, for letting me use this."

"Sure, Dan. Do you have your password to use getting in and out if you need a bathroom break?"

"Yes."

"Okay, make sure the door is locked when you leave. Happy hunting."

After he left, I sat down and logged on. The university subscribed to various advanced databases used by the various specialties. These were very expensive, and much more so because Centura was in an isolated location. Everything had to come in via satellite. I could never afford such links at home.

I got into the 'History Hunters' site and pulled up their search engine. I typed in "Robert Wilson," and added "freelance work gang organizer." No hits. Then I tried just the name and found 1,500 Robert Wilsons. Crap. It would take me all night to look those up.

I tried several different combinations of search parameters, but I seemed to jump back and forth between no results and too many to handle. I worked late into the night until I looked at my watch and saw that it was 1:00 a.m. Although I had told Marie not to wait up, I re-texted her and indicated I would be on an all-nighter. Then I lay down on a couch to rest.

I glanced upward to see Dr. Principi shaking me. "Dan, I said you could use my computer, not move in."

"Sorry, Dr. P, must have dozed off."

He handed me a cup of coffee, then walked over to the computer. "What do you have here?" He brought a list of my previous night's failed searches.

I joined him, sitting on the chair.

"Hmm … why don't you try Bob Wilson?"

"Why would anyone name their kid Bob?" But I typed it in and got 1,400 results.

"Now try Bob Wilson, Leaf Frog."

"He wasn't on their employee list."

"Try it anyway; he may have put it on a resume." After no results, he said, "Know anything about him?"

"Little. Mr. Greene said he was old then."

"Switch databases. Go to 'Registered Nursing Home Residents,' then repeat."

"Eureka! Three hits. Manageable."

"What you couldn't do all night I did in sixty seconds. That's why I'm a professor and you're a stupid orphan." Dr. Principi laughed at his corny joke while he shuffled toward his office.

After I quickly eliminated two of them, I found my man. Bob Wilson was a resident of the Fairlawn Manor, Greenville, Mississippi.

Chapter 6

"Yes, I'm the social worker here."

"I'm Daniel Kelley from Centura. I hear you have a Bob Wilson at your facility?"

"Yes, we do. Are you a relative?"

"No. My parents died when I was four, and I did not know them. I'm trying to look up people who knew my Dad, and I believe Mr. Wilson might remember him. Is he alert?"

"Bob? Oh yeah. Bob's as sharp as a tack, even still cuts a rug at our Saturday night dances."

"Do you think I could stop by and talk to him?"

"I'm sure he would love it, Dan. Bob has never had a visitor in the ten years I have been here. Just keep in mind that you may be treated like a celebrity; these folks treat any visitor like they were the president. You will be coming soon, won't you?"

"Yes, in a week or two. Why?"

"Bob is 102 years old."

Right after hanging up with the nursing home, my handcomp buzzed with another call. It was Dr. Principi. "Hello, sir."

"Dan?"

"Wait a second." I walked outside to escape from the racket the carpenters were making. "Hi, what's up?"

"What's up is I want you to come and get this crazy vehicle out of the warehouse. The guys over there are on me about the space it's taking up."

"That was a donation, was it not? What am I going to do with it?"

"No, the dean told me it was only a loan. And it's not my problem what you're going to do with it; they just want it out of there. Anyway, it's been attracting some attention lately."

"What attention?"

"Two feds were over here and wanted to look at it. They had a warrant."

"For what?"

"Just to search it."

"What did they say?"

"Nothing. They just looked at it and then left. Okay, so get it soon. And Dan, I don't have your graduate application yet."

"I'm working on it."

"Sure you are."

I had made arrangements with Wheeze to get the vehicle and bring it over to his house until we figured something out. So, about two days later, I had an awful day at work. I went over to fix a bad breaker switch at a lady's house, and the lady was so drunk that right in the middle of the job, she passed out and fell flat on her face on the basement floor. She was bleeding like a stuck pig and, after calling the rescue squad, I tried to hold a cold compress on her nose when she started to get sick all over the place. After a long chat with the paramedics, and an even longer chat with the police when they got there, the lady's husband came home and I had to listen to him. So, it was a great two and a half hours of me not making any money. I drove home smelling like cheap gin and vomit.

As I got out of my truck in my garage, Milt Frazer came pulling into our compound on his tractor with that amphibious vehicle behind on a trailer. Wheeze was following in his beat-up old pickup.

Milt got down off the tractor and met me walking toward him. He was not often in a good mood and today was no exception. "Okay, tattoo boy, here" he pointed toward Wheeze, "talked me into taking this contraption over to his house. Only his wife came out screaming that she didn't want it in the driveway. I thought she was going to bean me with a rolling pin. Then, I have to tote this thing another five miles over here. Now, Dan, where do you want it?"

"I don't know, let me ask Holden."

"Tell you what, if you don't tell me where you want it, I'm unhitching it right here."

"Okay, Milt. Can you back it in the new wing of the machine shed? I'll figure something out."

After Wheeze and I helped guide Milt into parking it in the shed, Ben Holden came out of his house and started in on me.

He said, "Dan, you can't put that in there. I have plans for that space."

I took several minutes to calm everyone, thank Milt and assure Ben, and then walked to my cabin.

Marie turned to me and asked, "Hi, honey. How was your day?"

The military airstrip at Thompson provided space for commercial flights in and out of Centura. There were only about two or three a day. Since most everything had to be supplied by air, large military cargo planes comprised most of the traffic. Marie, Diane Pine, Tom's wife, and the kids all made the trip to the airstrip to drop me off. Pat and Annie were interested in looking at the planes for about a minute, and then became more interested in a game of tag.

I was a veteran, and eligible for a military hop on one of the cargo planes, but couldn't arrange the connections for that day. I did manage to book one for the return flight home the next day.

I was lucky to get one of the new jets with the air pulse engines. While the military had been using them for years, commercial airlines had just started incorporating them into their fleets. Al Myers explained how they worked. A traditional jet engine sucked in air, ignited it, and then blew it out the back pushing the plane forward. The air pulse engine took in air, and then somehow expanded it using microwaves, making the volume of the air going out larger than the volume of the air coming in. This had the same effect of a jet engine, but used much less power.

The flight was incredible. There was no engine noise at all, only the wind that sped by outside. There was, however, a bit of shaking at altitude changes or outside air temperature fluctuations, but these only lasted a second or two. I even took a nap on the way to Memphis.

Memphis was a major hub for air traffic and the place was crammed with people. While I waited in line to walk off the plane, I checked my handcomp for my next gate. This is what I didn't miss about living in a large city: standing in line.

Walking out the gate, I saw her in an instant. It was Rose Russo, since I would recognize that face anywhere. My old friend and the girlfriend of my fellow Eagle, Jim Donovan, was walking at a brisk pace down the busy concourse. Dressed in a smart business suit, she looked like some sort of an airline executive. Her killer good looks were still evident.

She was walking so fast I could barely catch up with her.

"Excuse me, if it isn't Rose," I said.

She turned to look and slowed down. She smiled, "Well, hi there."

I expected a hug, or at least a handshake, but got neither while she continued to walk. "Can you imagine I just flew in from Centura?"

"Then you were probably on one of our new air pulse planes; how was the flight?"

"Great."

"I know a lot about Centura. My Dad was stationed at Thompson when he was in the Army."

I looked at her with astonishment, "I know. Rose, I'm Dan Kelley from Centura. You remember, Jim Donavan's friend."

"Well, sure you are." She kept walking.

"Ever hear from Jim?"

"Oh yeah. He's in Atlanta now."

We walked up to a door with a sign that said "Private," she grabbed the doorknob with her hand, and then looked at me. She seemed uncomfortable.

"I know he is, Rose. He's my business partner."

I studied her face while she kept inching closer to that door.

"Rose, you have no idea who I am, do you?"

She sighed like a weight had been lifted off of her. "Sorry, Jim had a lot of friends back then."

I was speechless. What the heck was going on here? I didn't want to cause any more agony for the poor girl, and said, "Well, okay then. Have a nice day."

"You too. Sorry." Then she disappeared behind the door.

I slowly continued on to my gate, and tried to make sense about just what happened. It was only eight or nine years since

I'd seen her. I knew I wasn't an exceptionally flashy or remarkable person, but we'd had heart-to-heart talks. How long did it take for me to fade away?

I had to take a puddle jumper from Memphis to Greenville. We encountered some rough weather and I was thankful when I heard the "cleared to land" announcement. I walked out to get a cab, and it was pouring rain with the temperature in the nineties. It was the first time I ever sweated during a rainstorm.

It would probably have been a better idea to get a hotel downtown. There was not much to do in the place I choose next to the extended care facility. However, the food in the restaurant was good and I liked watching the local news to hear the strange accents.

In the morning, the sky had cleared, the air was cooler, and a slight breeze blew out of the north. I walked across the street to the Fairlawn Manor. The block-lettered poster above Mr. Wilson's suite entrance that read "Welcome Dan" did little to prepare me for the greeting I received when I opened the doors.

All the residents either stood or sat around small tables in the main room of the suite. Suddenly they all clapped, cheered, or blew on party blowers and those paper air horns. Several tried to throw confetti, but couldn't get it very high in the air. Some had on cardboard party hats. A very slender, old man approached and took me by the arm. "Folks, I want you to meet my very dear friend, Dan, from up North."

I assumed this was Mr. Wilson, and let him lead me around to most everyone in the room for introductions. Most of the names I couldn't hear because of the noise in the room, and some of the residents couldn't hear me. After repeating my name to one woman in a wheelchair, she looked up at me and snarled, "Fran? What kinda dang name is that for a boy?"

I was then introduced to the charge nurse and the social worker, the latter assuring me that this was indeed Bob Wilson. They took pictures of Bob and me together.

"Mr. Wilson," I said.

"Call me Bob," he said with a big, although toothless, smile. Thick round glasses matched his completely bald head.

"Bob, is there a place we can talk alone?"

"Yeah. The sola-ruin."

I looked at the nurse for a translation and she repeated, "Solarium. At the end of the hall. Mr. Wilson has a distinctive vocabulary. You'll figure it out."

Bob then proudly announced to the room, "Dan and me are going to have a private talk."

He, with his cane, and I walked very slowly down to the sunroom. We sat on elegant wicker furniture while the old man smiled away, having the time of his life.

"Gotta admit, son, I don't know ya a-tall."

"Well, you might, Bob. I understand you used to work at the Leap Frog site, near Old St. Louis."

"Yeah. Yeah, I did. Long time ago."

"I think you may have met my Dad there. He was there too."

"Yer pap? Yer pap was there?"

"His name was Patrick O'Dea."

Bob began to laugh, "You e'spect me to know names? Son, I can't member when I peed last."

We both started to laugh. This Bob was a hoot.

"What did your pap do?"

"Odd jobs, fix-it stuff. General labor."

"I knowd most of them folks. I set up the work gangs, freelance guys, who worked for hourly wages. Mostly set up pre-fab buildings, cleared trees and brush. I worked for Mr. Gusto."

"Gustav?"

"Yeah. We called him Gusto. Don't remember no Patrick. Oh, wait, Patty? Used to sing to the cows?"

"Yes! Patty. You knew him?"

"Oh sure, I knowd Patty."

I wanted to hug the old man, my first eyewitness.

"He's yer pap? Quiet man, kept to himself. Had no use for most people. Rarely talked to him, only three, maybe four times."

"I thought you set up the general labor gangs. How come you didn't know him better?"

"Special guy. Took care of the cattle, lived out on the plains east of town, where the cows was. Fixed vehicles and worked dozers."

"Bulldozers?"

"Yep. Worked directly for Gusto mostly. Saw him on a dozer once, puttin' up some sort of berm, up on the north canyon. Saw 'em one other time fixing Gusto's duner."

"Duner?"

"Prairie runner, dune buggy. Patty was a dog, ya know?"

"Dog?"

"Prairie dog. Someone who can live off the land: hunt, trap, gather roots, and fruits. Had no use for people or their food neither. Aren't many true dogs, ya know."

"He had a family?"

"Oh yeah. Pretty little wife."

"Did you ever see her?"

"Only met her once. Quiet, just like Patty. Dark skin."

"Ever hear her speak?"

"No. Never spoke to me nor me to her. Had two baby boys. Yer pap was sure proud of those boys. Showed 'em off to me once."

"Bob, I'm one of those little boys."

"Get out!" He slapped my knee. "I held you once. I knew I knew you, son. I'll be dang."

"You must be getting tired, so I won't keep you long, Bob. I have just a few more questions. Did you know Mr. Kline?"

"Oh, yeah. He was the 'big cheese'. Mostly stayed in his office down by the river."

"How about Mr. Arthur Greene?"

"Army guy. Yep, knowd him too. Nice guy. Worked in getting us ready for inspection. Helped us workers out a lot. Brought us stuff."

"What stuff?"

"Oh, stuff. Equipment. Once he brought us some pumps to drain out some low spots. He did a good job there; he was a good man."

"I heard about pirates there. Was that true?"

"Oh, there was some. Not as many as people made out. The problems there was liquor, gamblin' and hoes."

"Excuse me. Hoes?"

"Prosatutes."

"Prostitutes?"

"Yep, them.

"Whatever happened to Gusto?"

"Oh, Gusto went up North, up the Mississip, to get two chainsaws my men left up there. Never came back. Some folks said he must 'a drove his duner in the river. The guy drove like a maniac. Always drove too fast."

"Do you remember Patty leaving?"

"He left too. One day he just up and left. Never knowd why. Didn't even know he was gone for a week or two after he left."

"So you don't know why?"

"Never knowd."

"Do you remember when he left?"

"Ah, don't remember any dates, son. Don't 'member much of the order of things happening. Too long ago."

"Were you there for the flood, Bob?"

"Oh, yeah. Awful. Came in the night like the wrath of God. Snowed all winter, rained all spring."

"How did you get out?"

"Rode on my mattress for a while, until it got soaked and sank. Then grabbed on the door to the rec hall and rode it, oh, twenty or thirty mile down the river 'til I grabbed on a tree trunk and climbed over to the shore. Dead bodies floatin' by me like a school of saugers. Saw Mr. Kline go by, eyes open, stone dead. Hoes and johns still in embrace, floatin' down to the hereafter together. It was a gruesome sight."

"One more thing I have to know, Bob. Patty, my pap, was he a good man?"

Bob patted my hand and smiled, "Patty was a good man. Don't take his antisocial feelin's as a bad thing. He never cared for men much but he never harmed anyone."

"Bob, thanks so much. I really have to get to the airport, but …"

"Hey, no. We got lunch for you. Yer stayin' for lunch."

The festivities continued in the main room. First, all the residents gathered for a group picture. Bob and I sat in front with him putting his arm around me. Then we had a surprisingly good lunch of ham, mashed potatoes, and some kind of peas I had never seen before. I then had to give a speech. Not sure what to talk about, I just described my family and life in Centura. I only spoke until two residents fell asleep, then I quit. Next came cake and ice cream. After I looked at my watch, and finally insisted on getting to the airport, most of the residents were sleeping right at the tables anyway.

Bob, now tired, sat in a wheelchair and slowly rolled along while we proceeded to the doors. Motioning me to bend down toward him, he gave me the most heart wrenching speech I had ever heard.

"You have no idea, son, how much this visit has meant to me. Don't fergit to write us and send pictures of your great family. Ya ever knowd what it's like, son? You ever knowd how it is to be put in a place where you didn't know anyone, and a place where no one ever visits you?"

"Yes, Bob, I once knew a place like that."

I hopped a Navy transport plane at the Greenville Airport that had stopped there to pick up a group of Marines bound for duty at Thompson. Since I was late, I had missed my opportunity to get a VIP seat in the front cabin, so I found myself sitting with the men in the cargo area. The soldiers crowded around me to get an answer to the famous question: "Was Centura as bad as everyone said it was?" I informed them of all the places to go and the ones to stay away from. For supper I was handed a field ration kit of refried beans and rice. At least it was a vegetarian meal that would make Marie very happy.

The Marines settled into private pursuits, and I reviewed the information I had received to date. I had recorded the conversation with Bob Wilson; however, I found that my voice recognition software did a pretty bad job of transcribing my friend's odd vocabulary. I had gotten some great clues, like my Mom was not only mute but now had dark skin. 'The Chaos' had taken interracial marriage from the avant-garde to a survival necessity. That was why people today had a golden brown tint to their skin. Few even noticed it, except for historians who were always looking at pictures of 'Old World' people in books. But Bob's experiences did not take place in antiquity, and for him to describe her being dark turned up even more questions.

The biggest problem, however, was his inability to remember dates or even what order events took place. Since he described my brother and me being babies, that memory must have been very early on in our stay there. When who did what was the vital information I needed. Also, was the flood scene exaggerated? Was the description of the prostitutes and their customers still being connected while they floated away realistic? Why, with such technology that they had at the time, did so many people get caught by surprise from that flood? Who left when? Every answer produced three more questions.

Even though I got home in the middle of the night, I was up at 5:00 a.m. with the goats milked by six. Tom Pine and his wife Diane joined us for breakfast. While we chatted over coffee, I related my encounter with Bob Wilson to everyone. Now that my Mom had been described with having dark skin, I began to wonder if she was even my mother. Annie and Patrick's skin tone matched mine and Marie's.

"It's not abnormal," Diane said, "darker skin still shows up in offspring, even generations later."

"How's Bo?" Marie asked Tom.

Tom had studied psychology through his master's degree before switching over to philosophy. He wasn't an expert, but he could understand the lingo the doctors spoke. "He's doing well and is becoming more animated."

"I sure would like to talk to him sometime about all those things he was saying up in that tree. The admitting physician told me she thought he had a purpose."

"Oh, I'm not sure about that," Tom went on. "But I'm bound to tell you that I don't think it's a good idea to rehash that moment with him."

"Why?"

"Have you ever heard of sealing over?"

"No."

"That's lingo for the recovery process. When the episode is over, the things he was experiencing get forgotten. This is a homeostatic response; it protects him. When you bring back the things he was verbalizing at the time, you bring back the underlying pathology that got him that way in the first place. Understand that what he was experiencing in his mind was absolutely terrifying. If he's forced to explain what he was saying, you bring back the demons that were saying it."

A rap on the front door got Marie up to go answer it.

"So, Dr. Pine, this whole process we're going through is very tiring. The closer I get to solving this puzzle, the further away I get. I don't know how I would ever write a history thesis."

Marie reentered the room, "So, dear, what did you do in Mississippi that I should know about?"

"Why?"

"The police are here, and they want to talk to you."

At the door I saw two military police officers with a pair of stern looks.

"Are you Daniel Kelley?"

"Yes."

"You'll have to come with us, sir. You are wanted for questioning."

"Can you tell me what for?"

"They didn't tell us."

"I think I have a right to know."

One of the MPs unsnapped the cover over his sidearm, and laid his palm on the butt of the gun. "Sir, I think you had better come with us. Right now."

Chapter 7

The officers patted me down and checked my identification, but didn't put me in handcuffs. That was a good sign.

As we drove up the road, one of them turned around to say, "We need to pick someone else up. A Salvatore Isaacs."

"Who?"

"Also known as The Wheeze."

"Wheezie? He lives over on South 2nd Street, down by the lake."

The policemen didn't talk much on the ride over. I had absolutely no idea what this was all about, although I considered every possibility. We approached Wheeze's small cottage and parked in the driveway.

I asked, "Hey guys, have you met this guy's wife?"

The officer in the passenger's seat turned toward me and shook his head.

"Maybe I should get Wheeze, just in case she's home."

"Is she violent?"

"Usually not, but she has sort of a problem with authority figures."

The officer just smirked at me and got out. When he approached the front of the car, suddenly the screen door burst open and all six feet, two inches, 240 pounds of Mrs. Wheeze came ambling down the front steps.

She crossed her arms, holding a potato masher in one hand with potatoes dripping off it. "What?"

The officer turned around, got back in the car, and said, "Okay, Kelley, we'll try it your way."

I started to doubt the reputation of the fearless military police.

I got out, but stood by the door. "Hi, Mrs. Wheeze."

"Dan, what trouble are you and Wheeze in now?"

"I'm not sure. They want us for questioning. I think he should come with us."

"Okay, if you say so," she turned her head to the side. "Wheeze, get out here!"

Wheeze exited the doorway, dressed in his customary black tee shirt and matching jeans. His eyes got big when he saw the police. He slowly started toward the car.

"Hey," his 'lovely' wife said, "I didn't get a kiss."

Wheeze had to get up on his tiptoes to kiss her.

She said, "Don't forget, if you get put in jail, call me, so I don't hold dinner for you."

Wheeze's sense of humor on the ride up to Thompson was not appreciated. "This isn't about that orphanage hall you burned down, is it, Kelley?"

"I didn't burn down any orphanage and I wish you wouldn't say things like that in front of the p-o-l-i-c-e. Okay, Salvatore?"

"Don't tell anyone about that."

We passed over the bridge and through the main gate, and noticed the base was as busy as usual. Almost as large as the town of Centura, Thompson covered several square miles and contained everything needed to sustain the personnel and families stationed there. Nearly everyone in the adjoining town, including Anchor Farms, did business with it.

The sitcom device in the squad car blared, "Unit fourteen."

Our driver responded, "This is fourteen."

"Take those subjects to the naval commander's office."

"Ten four."

Wheeze looked at me and I confirmed, "This could be bad."

We traveled down a street and came before a very stately building. Four white columns adorned the bright red brick structure that had a three-foot base of laid fieldstone. Our escorts brought us into the outer office of Captain Richardson's headquarters before they left. After the office manager showed us into the main office, we saw the captain sitting behind a desk as big as a battleship. Mrs. Henderson, Naval Intelligence Director, sat in front of the desk next to a gentleman in a business suit. Hopes of a glorious naval career seemed dim.

"Gentlemen, take a seat," Captain Richardson said. After he scrolled through a few documents on his deskcomp, the captain started to speak when his speakercom interrupted.

"Captain Richardson. There's a Ms. Hightower here. She says she represents the gentlemen."

He frowned, shook his head, and then responded, "Send her in."

The doors opened, and the 'blonde bomber' entered, spewing venom, "Okay gentlemen, I certainly need to start seeing some documentation here! Perhaps a warrant would be nice. Anyone ever think of that?" Ms. Hightower, one of Centura's leading trial attorneys, could both take your breath away with her beauty, yet shred you to ribbons with her tongue, and she knew full well she possessed both those traits. She came over to me and whispered, "Marie called me, said you got arrested."

"Ms. Hightower," Captain Richardson said, "we don't have a warrant because your clients were not arrested. They are wanted for questioning because we feel a Federal crime may have been committed..."

The gentlemen in the black suit quickly added, "...that may involve national security."

Ms. H. composed herself, sat down, and then turned toward me, "He's right you know." Then she looked at the captain, "Captain Richardson, with all due respect, sir, what's the deal sending the SWAT team over to pick them up? You know Dan Kelley, you could have called me and I would have brought him in."

"I know. Things got out of hand here. Mr. Durham, needing to question these fellows, called the M.P.s to bring them in, without my permission, by the way." He looked at the guy in the suit, "That is something he's promised never to do again!"

"I'm sorry, sir," he apologized.

"Okay, Mr. Durham, the floor's yours."

"Are you people familiar with the Defense Intelligence Agency?"

Wheeze blurted out, "Are you the guys that communicate with the aliens?"

Mr. Durham was speechless for a few seconds, then, "Ah, no, we're not those guys."

Captain Richardson chuckled, "Mr. Durham, perhaps you have not met 'The Wheeze'. He's a member of Centura high society. Some people would say on the fringe of society."

"That's me," Wheeze smiled.

I said, "You are the military's equivalent of the CIA. You guard against surprise attack, assist the military in operations, and so on."

"Correct," Mr. Durham said. "After recovering from 'The Chaos', and afterward, our 'Old World' satellites began to fail. Orbits decayed or they ran into space junk. We then sent up some new ones. My agency is in charge of looking after them. All currently functioning satellites now belong to the Department of Defense. Therein lays the instant concern. Mr. Kelley, I'm familiar with your story. I read this over the weekend." He pulled a plastibook hardcopy of Miller's book, Living on the Prairie, out of his briefcase. "Now, you and your folks were stuck out in the uninhabited region, south of here, in 3055, correct?"

"Yes, sir, and please call me Dan."

"Dan, who called the Marines to come and pick you up?"

"I always assumed my Dad did. There was a radio in our vehicle."

"Mr. Durham," Ms. Hightower objected, "he was four years old at the time."

"I know. I'll get to my point later. Now, you and 'The Wheeze' here returned to that site around 3070. Did either of you notice any strange electronics onboard? It would have to be a rather large, powerful transmitter."

We both shook our heads.

"Wheeze, you and some friends went down to retrieve the vehicle and bring it back up here. Then you restored it. During your work, did you notice anything of that nature?"

Wheeze responded, "No, like Dan said, just that radio."

"What kind of radio was it?"

"That little thing? I've seen newer versions on off-road vehicles I've restored, on Omnitrackers and the like. You know, guys used them on hunting and fishing trips when they go out of range of the cell tower. They're nothing but high powered walkie-talkies.

"Do you know what their range is?"

"Twenty, thirty miles tops and only if they're on flat ground."

"Where's that radio now?"

"The dump I guess. I took it out and installed a sound system. I need my tunes!" Wheeze stood up and started dancing around in a circle.

Mr. Durham frowned but Captain Richardson started to laugh.

Ms. Hightower calmed things down, "Wheeze, sit down, you're not helping matters."

"Did either of you know that the vehicle was stolen?" Mr. Durham continued.

"I object!" Hightower said, "Like I said ..."

Captain Richardson held up his hand, "Hold your horses. It was found to be missing from a demolition inventory years before. It was scheduled to be torn down for scrap metal so it was no big deal. We are not even implying that Dan's dad stole it, but he may have bought it off the black market."

I asked, "Do you want it back? My neighbors are complaining."

Captain Richardson shook his head.

"Okay, back to my real problem now," Mr. Durham continued. "As I was saying, the currently operating satellites are utilized by the military. We also rent broadband on them to quantanet service providers and satellite television networks. But we have to uplink the signals. Our commercial users send their signals to us; we encode them, send them up, and receive them at one of our towers. So, your emails have to be received by a tower here at Thompson before we send them out to you. Only the military, at designated facilities, can send and receive signals to the satellites."

"Dan," Mrs. Henderson took over, "when you gave a copy of that mission log of the helicopter to the captain, he gave it to me. In order to have it checked out I sent it to my main office in Atlanta. They sent it to the DIA."

"So what's the big problem here?" Hightower asked.

"It's this," Mr. Durham said. He pulled a copy of the message out of his case. "Do you see the code at the top of this message?"

"Yes."

"This is a string of numbers that, among other things, tells us the facility the message originated with. The code at the top of this one is counterfeit." Mr. Durham looked me right in the eye, "Someone hacked the satellite."

Ms. Hightower shot me the dirtiest look ever, and then looked at Mr. Durham, "Again, sir, my client was four at the time."

"I understand. I'm not suggesting anything related to these men. I just want you to know that this is very serious. Under certain circumstances, this could be considered an act of treason. I got a call from the Secretary of Defense last night, and she's very interested in this."

Ms. Hightower said, "This message has been laying here for over twenty years. Why has it taken you so long to come up with this?"

"We missed it. A message came in, it looked official, a helicopter was dispatched, and a person retrieved. We missed it because we were not looking for it. This has never happened in the history of the United States."

"Who did it?"

"No clue. We're running checks at every facility we have with this capability. It could be espionage or some soldier with a grudge."

"It's those darn aliens," Wheeze said, "I told you it was them."

"Here's my concern," I said, "we have a message here saying that a 'small band' of people were in peril out in the wilderness. You went down, picked up one, and then came back. My parents were out there! Why didn't you go back?"

The people in the room looked down.

Mrs. Henderson said, "Dan, you do know that everyone in this room was not there at the time."

Captain Richardson spoke, "No, I'm the ranking person in this room. This is my question to answer. Dan, I'm sorry, but it was probably indifference. You know the military never provided rescue services for those crazy enough to wander out into the uninhabited regions. The risk was all on the parties venturing out. I'm sorry, but your father was well aware of that risk or he should have been. There was a blizzard going on down there at the time. The crew probably felt that the risk to their lives did not justify further search."

Mr. Durham then said, "Dan, the captain has asked me to provide anything I can to help you solve the problem I read about. I'm really astonished that you got this guy to help you." He pulled up a copy of Myers' "O'Dea's Riddle." "This guy is brilliant. He's kind of a cult hero among the intelligence community."

"Who, Al?"

Durham looked at me with surprise and said, "Dr. Albert Myers? He won the Georgia Medal for Mathematics when he was twenty-two. And you call him 'Al'?"

"He's a friend of mine. I have his number here if you want to call him at the university. Ask for his assistant, Craig. He'll set you up with an appointment. He'd be flattered to know he's a cult hero. But please don't call him 'brilliant' to his face; we've already had to put larger doors in his cabin so he can get his head through."

Wheeze and I stood outside after the 'meeting' was over, and waited for Hightower. The cops had apparently driven off and now we had no way home.

Our gorgeous counsel came out, and I was just about to ask her for a ride, when she grabbed me by the shirt collar, "Okay, Kelley, is there anything you're not telling me?"

"No."

"I'm not kidding. Did you hear that in there? This isn't a schoolyard fistfight; this is major stuff here. I'm the best lawyer in town but even this is over my head. National security is no walk in the park, so you'd better be leveling with me. I want constant updates with whatever you and your wacky friends are up to. Got it?"

"Yes."

She let go of me and even tried to smooth out the wrinkles in my shirt, "Oh, and hey, you still owe me money. Am I ever going to see that?"

"For what?"

"For that thing I did, that hearing for Schlitz's nursing license."

I tried to joke, "Why, you didn't do anything."

"Oh no. You don't get out of it just because things didn't turn out in your favor."

"I'll have Holden send you a check."

"Thanks."

"Can we have a ride?"

She sighed. "Not all the way down in the boonies. Frank Davis is over at my office. I'll take you there and you can get a ride from him. Wait here, I'll get my car, by the way, it's a mess. I had to walk about a mile from here and I'm putting the walking time on your bill."

"Sh...eeze. What's up with her?" Wheeze said. He started to pace and ended up in front of a metal plaque on the wall of the building. "Wow, Kelley, this building was built in 2951, one of the first on the base. It's in the historical register."

"Wheeze, right now, I just don't care."

This didn't stop Wheeze who continued to read, "Hmm. Designed and built by Randall, Inc. Original fieldstone base cut and laid by August 'Vickie'."

"Who?"

"Now what mom in her right mind would name a kid after a month? April or June is okay, but …"

"What was the name on the stone work?"

"Ah, heck, I can't pronounce it."

I walked over to read it. I got a chill while I read "August Viche, Stone Mason."

Hightower's car was indeed a mess. Plastibooks, pamphlets, and reams of loose yellow legal-size paper were stacked in the back seat, with barely enough room for Wheeze to sit.

Her mood had mellowed during the ride to her office, "Sorry I got so excited back there. I don't even know why I keep you guys for clients. I think it's because you are such a challenge; you're always into something goofy and new. Just be careful, Dan, keep that Durham guy informed, send him texts, do whatever. Also, keep Mrs. Henderson and me up to date. You'll need to have documentation of revelations while they unfold. Keep people in the dark and I may end up trying to convince a jury after the fact."

"Okay. How's Frank Davis working out?"

"Good. I have him back doing investigative work. He's certainly overqualified but that's all I have. I've been trying to get him to start something in estates or taxes, maybe even make him a partner someday. But he insists on just doing some mindless work for a while. That crappy marriage deal really threw him for a loop."

"I keep trying to get him out some, do a little casual dating. He doesn't like the outdoor stuff too much that we're all into."

Hightower laughed, "He reminds me so much of you, Kelley. He's an all or nothing, one woman-man. He'd be great a husband, but makes a terrible casual friend."

Things were heating up and getting interesting regarding this mystery. Such was evident during the impromptu genealogy meeting I called. I could see renewed interest in the eyes of our members. Even Ben and Angie Holden were attending. I gave a brief introduction of my findings to date and stated that I would be posting my transcripts and notes in our shared files to our secure site on the quantanet cloud.

Our chairperson, Dr. Al Myers, then took over. "Okay, Dan, before you do that, I want to let you all know that I've instituted a change. Currently, we have all this committee's materials on a cloud site. I've set up a transponder and our own server in the techroom of the bunkhouse. I'll give you all an access code and password. You will only be able to connect to it when you are around the compound here. I'm going to take all of our stuff down from the cloud and keep it here on a local intranet."

"Do I sense paranoia in our chairperson?" Ben asked.

Al smiled, "In a word, yes. It's this Mr. Durham. He does appear to have good intentions and I feel he can help us with this O'Dea project, but something he said to me during our meeting got me to thinking."

"Do you think he's able to see our stuff on there?" I asked.

"I think he may have already read it."

Clyde added, "Can he do that? Doesn't he need a warrant or something?"

"I think he can do just about anything if national security is the issue. I'm not exactly sure he did, but I would feel better if we control what he sees. I have his number and I can forward any physical evidence we come across. I'm not interested in withholding evidence, just our speculations, and our theories. Okay? Anything else?"

"Yes," I said. "Al, I want to check something out. Do you remember when we were down at 'Destination E', and you were taking all sorts of measurements and such? You mentioned that you could order satfotos of the area, now that we knew where it was. Could such a thing be done?"

"Sure, what are you interested in?"

"I want two. I want a picture of our compound now and one of it before we developed the site. Say about ten years ago."

"Why?"

"I want to check out some compass headings. I'm especially interested in my cabin and that tall pine tree, southeast of my cabin. The one Schlitz scaled."

"Sure, no problem."

"Can you explain the process to me?"

"Sure. The university has a contract with a company that makes up those images. You see, satellite pictures of the whole country, even the uninhabited areas, are taken all the time. They are very wide shots but are stored with all the detail in them. What this company does is take the wide shot, find the spot with the global coordinates you supply, focus in on that spot, and come up with a detailed photo. For example, remember the drone that took pictures of Mount Rushmore to show us that George Washington's nose fell off? Now to verify that, one could ask for a satfoto. So the wide-angle shot would be a huge area, say both North and South Dakota. Then the company would take that and focus down on that spot to come up with a photo of George's head, or even so close one could examine the pores in the rock. These photos are able to provide much more detail than anything available for free on the quantanet. They even have an infrared mode."

"Who takes the wide-angle photo?"

"Oh, the military does those."

I ended with "Okay, thanks."

Al concluded by saying we would meet again in a few days after everyone had digested my latest material.

After the meeting, I was on the phone to Dr. Principi. This crazy gut feeling I had gotten when I saw the name of that stone mason was intriguing me to come up with more information about him. Perhaps this was a wild goose chase since this guy was around 126 years ago. When I asked Principi about the best database to look up a person who helped construct the Thompson Defense Base, he referred me to the military historian at the base library.

When I called the library office, a young lady invited me up to meet with the historian.

The next day, with a break between calls, I hopped over to the base library. When I entered the main room of the small library, I saw that a class was in progress. The young woman I had talked to turned out to be a petty officer third class, and the historian a rather brash young Navy ensign. The students were a mix of base military personnel and a couple of students from the university, apparently sent over here for some military course. The teacher, obviously very smart, was a jerk. He enjoyed going around the room with questions for the fun of embarrassing his students when they didn't know the answers. I immediately noticed that he must have gone to the same teaching school as Dr. Phillips.

"So," 'Mr. Smarty Pants' went on, "who can tell me the one key personal factor that helped Napoleon survive during his humiliating retreat from Moscow in the winter of 1812? Anyone?" He looked around the room, but everyone was too intimidated to respond. He then saw me in the back and said, "Perhaps our visitor would like to attempt a guess."

It was a grossly simple question, but I didn't want to tick him off by showing him up. However, with everyone looking at me, I felt I had no choice. "He kept his horse alive."

"Excuse me?"

"He kept his horse alive, sir."

"No, that's not what I meant. He faced certain starvation and a few good meals of horsemeat would go a long way. Care to change your answer?"

"No, sir. It wasn't a top priority. He knew he could go two or three weeks without eating. But he also knew that he would be dead in two days if he had to walk in that snow."

"Well, class, seems you all just got taught a lesson by an employee of Ron's Electrical. That is the correct answer. Ever think of majoring in history, sir?"

"I get that question more than you know, sir."

"Okay, class dismissed." He looked at me, "I'll have King show you how to navigate our system here since you seem capable of doing your own search." He retreated to a private office off the rear of the room.

After the room cleared, Ms. King shook my hand, "Petty Officer King, History Technician."

"Dan Kelley, history major, by the way. Your boss is a real charmer."

"Oh, he's just holding a grudge with the Navy for transferring him here. He's not too bad. So, you're interested in the weird stone mason. I looked him up before you got here and he's quite a character. This won't take long."

In fact, PO3 King had found less than a page of text of information on him. I quickly transferred it to my handcomp along with some examples of his art.

Ms. King then asked my opinion on a problem she was having. She had three years of college history and indicated that if she could finish her B.A., she could then get a master's degree in military history that would make her eligible for a commission. I gave her contact information for Dr. Principi. He could certainly take care of her B.A. here and may be able to get her into an online program for the military part of it.

Later that day I stopped at my old alma mater, the Centura Orphanage, to get information on the other Viche, all of which would be presented at our next meeting.

On the next sunny Sunday afternoon, the family and I went down to the lakeshore. The new house I was wiring was a lakefront home and, since I knew it had not been sold, we borrowed the beach for the afternoon. With the lake water still too cold for swimming, the kids were content with exploring items washed up on the Lake Michigan shore. Marie had invited a nurse she worked with and I talked Frank Davis into coming along also. Our attempt at matchmaking, however, was a disaster since the two appeared to show little interest in each other.

After we returned home and our guests had departed, I cooked a family meal on the homemade grill. Corky and I had constructed a stone oven/fireplace out of fieldstone for family use. Cooking over a wood-fueled fire was a skill I learned back in the days when we were in the wild. A more complicated process compared to using charcoal, wood logs had to be reduced to glowing coals before actual cooking could begin, and the fire fed constantly to maintain an even temperature. I was under the mistaken impression that Annie really loved my cooking. However, I soon realized that finishing all her vegetables meant dessert, and dessert meant ice cream.

We gathered that evening in the machine shed. Besides Ben and Angie, Wheeze was also there. Al Myers called the meeting to order.

He said, "Okay. We now have had time to review some new and startling information. In summary, we now have contact with a current Centura resident who was at the site. Although Mr. Greene did not know Dan's dad, he will be valuable in confirming issues that arise. A 102-year-old nursing home resident in Mississippi confirmed Mr. O'Dea's existence. He has also verified that Dan is a real boy."

Wheeze interrupted, "I don't think we can rule out Kelley being an alien yet. He does act kind of weird."

"Ha. Ha. Ha." I monotoned, "you guys are so funny."

Al continued, "Patrick O'Dea worked as a laborer for the deputy site director. We also know that Lilly, Dan's mom, has been described as having dark skin. In addition," Al pointed at the vehicle that now took up most of the room, "we have learned that this vehicle was stolen."

"Speaking of that 'Beast'," Ben said looking at Wheeze and I, "have you guys figured out a place to put it yet?"

We shook our heads. Al and Ben did not know it at the time, but they had just come up with our new nickname for the vehicle.

Al said, "Anything else new to add to the case?"

I raised my hand and said, "I found out some interesting information. Up at the base the other day, I noticed one of the men who worked on the original construction was a stone mason by the name of August Viche. This is interesting because he has the same last name as Governor Viche, my first roommate at Delk Hall, who met his demise at the hands of the Mustangs. He apparently built the fieldstone base to the naval commander's headquarters building. Research also revealed that he added decorative stonework around the parade grounds and at the bases of several flagpoles. He did most of his work in 2951 through 2953. Then it gets interesting. He and an associate sculpted several hundred octagon shaped flagstones and placed them on both sides of the road that ran around the perimeter of the base. This is now named Perimeter Road. I'm sure you guys know those stones."

Ben and Al looked at each other and shook their heads.

Clyde saved me by saying, "I know the road, Dan, and the stones. Please go on."

"Well, a conflict then broke out. The Department of Defense denied they even ordered the project and wouldn't pay August for the work. After he threw a raging fit before the military commanders, August walked off the job leaving several projects unfinished. Now get this. He and his associate disappeared without a trace. They were never listed on any departing flights back down south. One witness described the last time they were even seen as '... walking down the beach along Lake Michigan in a southerly direction ... wearing backpacks.'

"So, we now switch to contemporary times. A Governor Viche was admitted to Delk Hall of the Centura Orphanage on August 14, 3056. He attended Centura High School for one day, and then dropped out, never to return to school. He was probably shunned by everyone for his grotesque physical deformities. A year or so later, near his eighteenth birthday, a committee decided to continue Gov as an adult border. Residents are normally discharged from the orphanage when they reach adult status, but I'm sure they felt sorry for him for not having a place to go. He then worked a series of odd jobs and I found one arrest for vagrancy. He was discharged from the orphanage on September 9, 3063, reason: death. Here, however, is the interesting part taken right from his file, 'Birthplace: Unknown, Date of Birth: Unknown, Birth certificate on file: No.' Creepy. One Viche goes off into the unknown, and one hundred years later one comes back from the unknown."

"So what's your point?" Al asked.

"Doesn't this sound odd?"

"But I fail to see the relevance. So what?"

I squeezed my pen so hard I almost broke it from Al's assertion of insignificance. Plus everyone just sat there, and stared at me with these blank looks. Tom Pine, however, was giving me that small controlled smile of his he often got when I was on to something.

He said, "Al, one of the rules of this committee is that we consider all hunches. I suggest we add Dan's research to the file for future reference if so required."

"Agreed. Dan, upload it." Al looked around the room, "Okay, anything else before we speculate?" Getting no responses, he proceeded, "We have entered a new phase of this case. Sure, we still don't know a number of how's and why's. A new entity has been introduced. A distress call was initiated and transmitted to Thompson Defense Base when Patrick O'Dea's vehicle broke down. We don't know by whom, although we know who it wasn't. It didn't originate at Thompson. Why would they send a satcall to themselves? Old St. Louis had no such capability. We know Patrick didn't send it because he did not have the intelligence for such a feat. No offense, Dan."

"None taken, Al."

"Do you guys even know the nearest military installation with the capability of sending such a transmission?" Al scrolled through his screenpad, "It's Arnold Air Force Base, south of Nashville, Tennessee. Now, who would know that Patrick was in trouble, call Arnold, and then have them transmit? What we have here is Occam's razor in reverse. We have several complicated and unlikely scenarios that attempt to explain events, but no simple ones."

Wheeze said, "I know I've been joking with you guys about aliens, but I hate to admit that I have the best option going here."

We all smiled, while Al added, "I tend to agree with you, Wheeze. I also hate to make this next statement. Guys, we cannot rule out any super intelligent entity here, even the U.S. government."

"You think Patrick O'Dea may have been some sort of agent?" Angie asked.

"He could have worked for any government, foreign or domestic. Anyway, he fits the profile. He was quiet, kept to himself, and had a wife who spoke little, if at all."

"But kids?" Clyde asked. "You don't often hear of a spy running around the wilderness with two babies."

"Kelley has two kids," Angie added. "Hmm, maybe he's a spy too. I say we put him under the lights and interrogate him."

"So what do we do now?" I asked, ignoring Angie.

Tom Pine took the floor, "I said this eight years ago, and I'm saying it again now. I felt something down there on that hill at good old 'Destination E', Patrick O'Dea's final stop. I think our answer is down there and I think it deserves another look."

"So, how do we get there? I don't fancy another hike," Ben said.

Wheeze got up, walked over to the "Beast" and placed his hand on it. "Anyone want to go for a ride?"

116

Chapter 8

Al said, "It would be nice to ride."

"I've rebuilt and restored most of it," Wheeze said. "It has a new auxiliary solarskin, and I've rebuilt the CVT. I took the traks off the back and put on big muddies and brand new axles. We have optional two, four, or six wheel drive."

"But we're missing three, not so minor, items," Ben added. "We need a decent motor, a bank of lithium-ion batteries, and a solar inverter."

"The chemistry department has all sorts of long-term storage batteries," Al said, "and I can get my hands on them."

Wheeze acted like a kid in a candy shop and said, "I read an article the other day that some folks up at the university built this state-of-the-art electric motor. It's a beefy boy, all double gauged with a sealed lubrication system. If I had that, we could 'book'."

"Where's it kept?" I asked.

"Electrical Engineering, I think."

Tom Pine and I looked at each other. He said, "Well, that's Dr. Phillips' shop and he hates my guts. Dan said he called me a wacko the other day. I can't help you there."

"I'll get the motor," I said.

Tom turned around to look at me, "He doesn't think much more of you either."

"I know his weakness."

Clyde was looking at his computer, and then said, "And the Army's got solar inverters right up there in the warehouse. I'll have to pay for it though. I'm assuming this is a venture we're going to invest in?"

Ben assured, "I think it's a done deal. I'll put it out on all handcomps of the partners for a vote, but I'm sure it will be approved. Let's get those major things first, then meet again to discuss who is going and what we need to bring. We will all be needed around here until we get the crops and tomatoes planted, so we have some time."

Clyde added, "And let's keep this quiet. Nobody outside Anchor Farms partners, Tom, Diane, and the Wheezes need know about this."

Ben added, "We'll need to inform Hightower sometime, but no need of that until we have more definite plans."

After the meeting was adjourned, I couldn't escape a couple of small discussions that prevented me from getting back to the cabin and talking to Marie. By the time I got into the house, blabbermouth Angie had already called Marie to spill the beans about the trip. I found my wife pulling stuff out of a storage closet.

She handed me my old animal skin backpack I had used on my previous trip, and said, "You're going to need this I suppose."

"You know, Marie, I don't really have to go."

"Are you kidding? This whole trip is for you, and long overdue, by the way."

"But the kids are so small."

"Diane Pine and I have already talked about this. She doesn't want to go this time, but I'm sure Tom does. She's going to be staying here with me. Actually, Tom has been wondering for a few years now why you haven't been more interested in this."

"It just seems like an excuse. 'O'Dea's Riddle' may be unsolvable. I may be wasting my, and everybody else's, time. I should be putting it out of my mind, but I keep it in front of me and am using it like a barrier to keep from moving on."

"I don't see it that way. I certainly don't see you not moving on with anything. This is a search for you, your identity, just as much as it is a search for your parents. I see you on that hill over there. I see you staring down south. You're quiet about it but your mind is working. I just know that I now have two-thirds of a husband. You have to make me one promise."

"What's that?"

"Bring the whole one back."

The next morning, I drank hot, black coffee and watched the sunrise from our back patio. I always loved listening to the forest wake up. The birds were the only alarm clock I ever needed. It usually started with a few tweets just before sunrise, and then the chirping turned into all out mayhem by six. Details raced through my mind, however, on this morning. I fought them off and concentrated on my handcomp and my agenda for the day. Just then a call came in.

"Dan? Durham from the DIA. Hope I didn't wake you."

"No sir, good morning."

"I got some interesting news here on your mother. I finally found your parents' marriage certificate, and things just keep getting stranger. They were married in Birmingham, Alabama. Your dad was born in Florida, his parents deceased. Now get this, your mom's maiden name is listed as Lilly O'Dea."

"So you're saying my Dad married his sister?"

119

"No. It could be a distant relative or just coincidental. Both her parents are listed as unknown. Also, in the 'place of birth' slot is listed United States of America. No town or no state or territory is listed. I'm surprised that Alabama accepted this. The person who married them was certified clergy, however, and legally allowed to marry people. His name was Armand White Feather."

"That sounds Native American. I wasn't aware there were any organized Native American religions left."

"I wasn't either, but I'll check around for Mr. White Feather."

"Any news on that other problem you told me about?"

"I can't talk about that on the phone. Check in with Mrs. Henderson on that. I have to run to a meeting now. I'll be in touch."

As I began my drive up to the university, I thought about how the words "deceased" and "unknown" kept showing up everywhere. I recalled when the orphanage issued me a certificate of discovery; this was before anyone here knew who my parents were. They gave me the name Daniel Kelley and a fake birthday with the words, "On or about" written after it. In the place for my parents' names they had "Undetermined/missing." Then when I went to file for a corrected certificate, with the name Daniel O'Dea, the court wouldn't accept it because I still had no proof. They wouldn't accept my brother's word of mouth. Heck, maybe my parents weren't even Patrick and Lilly O'Dea, and maybe my brother is the alien Wheeze was talking about.

I had to wait a good hour for my old friend Professor Phillips to show up. I had to remember to become a department chair since they could come to work whenever they wanted.

"Well, Mr. Kelley, good morning. I'd ask how the family is but I'm afraid you would start yelling at me again."

"Sorry, Dr. Phillips, it was a bad day. I need a favor."

"What?"

"You guys put a prototype electric motor together last winter. I want to borrow it for a while."

"That big thing? You could run a tank with that. You can't put it in a car; it's illegal."

"It's for off-road."

"Do you know how much that thing costs?"

"I know what it would be commercially. But I also know you put it together with spare and donated parts. Plus you used graduate students to do the work. I also know no auto company wants it because it would cost too much to mass-produce. So I would say it's practically worthless."

"What do you want it for?"

"I want to take my family on a summer vacation out on the prairie."

"I'm not in the mood for your humor today, Kelley."

"I really need it, sir."

Dr. Phillips leaned back in his chair and thought for a minute. I knew I had him then. He smiled, "Well, I'm thinking something could be worked out here."

I pulled my handcomp out of my jacket pocket and projected a holo-image on the wall. "This is my written intent to apply for your master's program in electrical engineering. I can't say I'll start your undergraduate prerequisites this summer, but certainly in the fall..

121

"Well, this is interesting. We may not have to apply that underachiever label to you after all."

"Let's get one thing straight here, Dr. Phillips. I'll give you due and proper respect with your being the department chair and you know my record at this university. I received a high school diploma and an associate's degree in electricity, simultaneously, when I was eighteen. I earned another associate's in philosophy a year later, and most recently a bachelor's in history. I'm a veteran, I got a wife, two kids, two cars, a house, a full partnership in two businesses, and I've had a 4.0 average since the fifth grade. I'm not going to take this underachiever crap from you or anyone else! Are we clear on that, Dr. Phillips?" I ended with pointing my finger in his face.

He sat back in his chair with a stunned look. "Well, seems I underestimated you, Mr. Kelley. This is the first time a student has yelled at me during an admission interview." He looked at my written statement. "We can take care of this right now." He typed "disapproved" at the bottom, then electronically signed it, and looked at me. "I don't know where your heart is, Kelley, but it's certainly not in electrical engineering. I hope it's at least over in history."

"Dr. Phillips, I need that motor."

"It's over in the warehouse; you can pick it up tomorrow. Try and get it back here in the fall. If not, well, I'll tell the dean it blew up or something. That's all, Mr. Kelley."

I picked up my handcomp and walked to the door. "Thanks, Dr. Phillips."

He did not respond.

Tom Pine's lectures definitely have some value, I thought, while I drove to the military base. At times, it helps to analyze someone's simple statement to discover the important phrase.

I walked into Mrs. Henderson's office, and she greeted me warmly with, "Hey Dan, staying out of trouble?"

"Doing my best, ma'am." I took a chair in front of her desk. "Mr. Durham called me this morning but told me I would have to get updates from you. What's new?"

"You have an unsecure phone; that is why. Well, we didn't find any evidence that some military guy at one of the transmission stations hacked in. I'm not even sure why they wasted their time checking that."

"Why not?"

"Every transmission has a sending facility code written right into it on the ground. The quantanet computer puts it in there and there is no way to get around that. It's like an IP address on a handcomp. Also, your dad couldn't have reached any facility from where he was. In fact, we have no evidence he called anyone."

"So what are we looking at now?"

"What we feared most: an outside party. Either your father called another person or such a person observed his plight. Either way that would mean someone was within a reasonable proximity of where he broke down."

"Wheeze's alien?"

Mrs. H smiled, "Sadly, that's the best hypothesis we have right now. To make matters worse, it all happened twenty years ago. The nearest people to the site, with the exception of Centura, were the Old St. Louis folks. We checked out Kline, Greene, and Gustav and none of them that much computer savvy. The rogue pirates we prosecuted didn't either, and in none of those cases was there any evidence of anyone ever going as far out to the east as your parents did. Leap Frog had a computer specialist there, but he drowned in the flood. Why do you think your dad left?"

"My only guess is some kind of workplace squabble Dad and Gustav got into."

"If you were in your dad's shoes, under what circumstances would you have risked the lives of your family and made such an exit?"

"I don't know, why do you ask that?"

"Sometimes it helps, with close relatives, if you try to think like them."

"My biggest fear is that he was mixed up with the pirates."

"From all the knowledge I have about him that seems unlikely."

"I sure hope so. Well, thanks, Mrs. H, I'll be around if you need me." I didn't tell her that I might not be around.

Wheeze and I loaded the motor on his truck the next day. We made sure it was well padded and secured in the bed. While we smiled and laughed all the way down to our compound, Wheeze could hardly contain himself. His restoration business dealt primarily with recreational and off road hydrocarbon powered vehicles, and this project was the ultimate.

"I probably should have done some closer measurements," he told me, "as I believe we are going to need a shoehorn to get this baby into the motor compartment."

"Where is that?"

"It's right behind the front seats, in the floor. The underbody is sealed, and since we'll be in the rivers when crossing, we'll have to go in through the roof."

After we arrived at the machine shed, I did something I had not done in a long time and looked over the "Beast". Wheeze had matched the auxiliary solarskin camouflage pigment perfectly. Three axles held up our UXU with large mud-gripping tires. The front end looked much like a truck cab on top, and had a bottom that tapered down to facilitate locomotion in water. There were two doors on each side with two hatches on top and a large door in the rear of the vehicle. The interior rear of the vehicle looked like it had been used to transport troops, although someone had converted it into a living space. Two propellers surrounded by debris guards extended from the rear.

We had to take part of the removable roof off to drop the motor in with a chain hoist. The installation was rather easy, by merely bolting it to four engine mounts. Wheeze easily connected the driveshaft to the transmission. A simple switch mounted on the dashboard switched power from the wheels to the propellers.

Wheeze was smiling ear to ear while he looked over his work. "Once Clyde gets here with the solar inverter and Al with the batteries, you get to wire it, Mr. Kelley."

I looked over the wiring schematic that was with the motor, while Wheeze went to get the manuals that were in the UXU when we found it. He returned to see me scratching my head.

"Dan, you look like you don't have a clue as to what you're doing."

"I haven't done that much with solar, maybe in the Navy, and never on a vehicle. These instructions are nothing more than graduate student lab notes, even the diagrams are drawn free hand."

"Well, I have a suggestion. I have a friend, 'Outlaw'. That's what everybody calls him anyway. He wires vehicles for me and does his own motorcycles. He's a whiz at wiring. Why don't I have him come over one day this week and you two can do this together?"

"Okay, how about Wednesday? I have to watch the kids for a while now, and I still need to get a few jobs in today. I'll take the motor wiring plans and look them over. The batteries and solar inverter should be here tomorrow, and Wednesday I'll clear my whole day for this."

"Sounds good."

I returned to the machine shed at 6:00 a.m. on Wednesday to find Wheeze already working. I saw the new battery bank and solar inverter globe sitting next to the wall. Wheeze had the cowl cover off and was tinkering with the interior of the controls.

"Are we going to take it off the trailer?" I asked.

"We might leave it right on here because we'll need to take it over to the river for a test float."

I took a closer look at the rooftop solar chargers, which supplied the motor power, and noticed six bullet-shaped domes about a foot and a half in diameter. The tops were covered with a thick red plastic.

"So, we don't need one of those metallic satellite dish-looking panels?" I asked.

"No, these are the newest thing. Apparently, they are made like a two-way mirror, allowing sunlight to go through the red covering, but prevented from exiting. The light is reflected off mirrors in there, bounces around, and then becomes focused on a metal bar in the middle. The energy goes down to the base where it's converted to electrical current, then on to the batteries. After you guys are done wiring, I'll fabricate some brackets to hold them to the roof. They are much more efficient than that tin foil panel your dad had on here."

The new batteries were also much smaller than conventional models. Everything we were putting into the "Beast" seemed top shelf.

"Wheeze, when is your friend going to be here?"

"Any minute. Dan, I want you to know that 'Outlaw' is kind of weird."

"You scare me when you think someone is weird. Weird how?"

"Well, he doesn't talk much. He never finished high school. Plus, he's done some time."

"Do you mean at the detention center, the Irish Fort?"

"No, more like the South Carolina State Prison."

"Wheeze! I have kids around here. What did he do?"

"I'd rather not tell you. He's done his time and he's all rehabbed. It's only for the day."

Before I could protest further, this huge hulk wearing a World War I German Army helmet rode up to the shed on this stretched-out chopper. He was dressed in a black leather vest, unbuttoned and shirtless, with black leather pants and boots.

After he dismounted and walked into the shop, I held out my hand to shake, but he just walked by me muttering, "Hey." He went straight over to the "Beast" and I noticed this slight smile on his face when he looked at it. The "Beast" sure was popular with the working class.

All of my reservations disappeared, however, when I saw this guy work. I mainly pulled wires through the body of vehicle while he made the connections. He never looked at a schematic once. He would grab a handful of wires in complete disarray and connect them so fast, I couldn't tell how he knew what one went to what connection.

At lunchtime, Wheeze and I ate a sandwich while 'Outlaw' continued working while he munched on a power bar. Chuckling to myself, I thought about how institutions like the Centura Orphanage and people like Dr. Phillips missed noticing people like this. This guy was a genius at what he did, and no one would ever know seeing him on the street.

We finished about two in the afternoon. Outlaw plugged an AC/DC converter into an outlet and the whole vehicle lit up. We had headlights, fog lights, searchlights, and even taillights. The interior had dashboard lights, cabin lights, and even a small refrigerator kicked on. The "Beast" was alive.

Outlaw was getting ready to leave, when I grabbed my handcomp to transfer him some money.

He walked up to me, shook my hand, and said, "Thanks for letting me work on this," and walked out.

As he rode off, I said to Wheeze, "Didn't he want any money?"

"Probably not. He likes money; he just has a very inexpensive lifestyle. Don't worry about it; he was doing me a favor."

I left the machine shed for the day and passed Tom Pine, Ben, and Angie Holden coming in for the evening shift to work on the "Beast". I was preparing to sit down for dinner when Ben put out a group message for an emergency meeting of the genealogy committee. Heading back into the shed, I saw everyone standing around Wheeze and looking at a pamphlet he was holding.

"I can't believe I never noticed this before," Wheeze said.

"What's up?" I asked.

Tom looked at me, "Dan, what's the one new thing you came out with during your hypnosis session?"

"Ah, gee. Can't think of ..."

Tom continued, "Get the book."

Wheeze said, "So, what is the first thing you would do if your solar panel blew off and you had to put it back on?"

After it hit me, I said, "You get out the manual for the solar panel!"

"What page do you go to?"

"Troubleshooting and repair."

Wheeze showed me the manual, opened to that page. It had a note, written in pencil that read, "Broke down, only two miles from target. Will make repairs, get to target, and then home."

"I'll have to do a formal comparison, Dan, but I believe that's Patrick's handwriting," Tom said.

"How did we miss this?"

Wheeze responded, "Don't you remember? When we first found the "Beast" you took the manuals out of the storage compartment and handed them to me. They were in plastic covers. I didn't think the manuals had ever been taken out, but I see they have a re-sealable closer."

Ben Holden added, "This proves that the solar panel came off while you were all still in the vehicle. I'm sure your dad wanted to save his remaining power, so he jotted down this note instead of using the voice log on the OBVAI. He would have probably dictated it once he had a power source again. But wait, that's not all."

Ben opened a second manual, the one for the vehicle itself, and turned to the back to a section where an owner could keep a log of maintenance tasks performed. There seemed to be several entries made by military personnel, but Ben ran his finger down the page and stopped at one that appeared to be in my father's handwriting. It read, "2/4/55 – new vehicle arrived, axels in need of lubrication, will inform owner."

Ben was ecstatic, "Your dad worked on this vehicle. It had arrived in February of 3055, a few months before he left Old St. Louis. Plus it proves he didn't own it when it arrived. Somebody else did. He bought, borrowed, or stole it while he was there."

Clyde offered, "I think this shows that this trip wasn't something he was planning for a long time. Something came up between February and August of that year that prompted his departure."

"I don't think this proves anything," Al said. "How do we know it wasn't that back track that was busted instead of the solar panel?"

Wheeze answered, "Why would he have the manual for the solar panel out if it was a track? Plus, he wouldn't need to have his wife come out with him to fix a wheel. One man could fix that with a jack and a few hand tools."

"Well, I think we need a bit more tangible evidence before we go jumping to conclusions," Al said. "This does show, however, that he was headed back to Old St. Louis as soon as he made that last stop. Why else would he have written 'and then home' because we all know that home was at the Leap Frog site?"

We stood around and talked for about an hour. Al was very smart and all, but sometimes he could be a pain in the neck. Al and Isaac Newton could be twin brothers. Neither could assume the presence of gravity without an apple falling on their heads.

This whole situation was wreaking havoc on my thinking. I thought about it with coffee in the morning; I thought about it at night before falling asleep. The subject also visited me at various times during the day. I looked forward to doing electrical jobs for a respite. Working with electricity didn't allow for daydreaming.

We planted the remaining garden crops later that week, and it proved to be a wonderful diversion. I loved working outside. However, while I drove our tractor pulling Milt Frazer's seed drill up and down the field, my mind soon wandered back to Lilly and Patrick O'Dea, prairie nomads. One time the drill jammed, and I went about twenty feet without planting anything. A sudden charge across the field by a cursing Milt and Clyde finally brought me back to reality.

After a couple of days, we had twenty acres of oats and another twenty of alfalfa in the ground, more than enough for our livestock.

At the end of the second day, Clyde drove and I rode back on the tractor to the machine shed and pulled the drill inside. Ben was there to greet us.

"Good job, guys," Ben thanked us. "That will keep the cows happy during the winter."

We watched Frank Davis pull up next to the bunkhouse in his new car. "Clyde," he said after he walked up to us, "looks like you and Kelley need a shower."

Clyde joked, "I am 'one with the earth,' all right. It's all over me. So, Frank, how's the job?"

"That's what I came down here to talk to you about. I don't work there anymore."

"Why?" Ben asked.

"I got fired."

We all looked at him, stunned.

Ben asked, "Hightower fired you? That doesn't seem likely. What happened?"

"I broke company policy about romantic relationships within the firm."

I said, "Man, give it a while. You've only been working there a month. Who was it, that court reporter?"

"It's that new lawyer she hired," Ben added, "that's who it is."

"No."

"It's not the receptionist, is it Frank?" asked Clyde. "You sure she's over eighteen?"

"It's none of them. It's the owner."

All three of us in unison, "Hightower?" You could have knocked us over with a feather.

"I can't believe it. I mean Hightower is so, so formal," Ben gasped.

Clyde added, "We don't even know her first name. She signs all her documents C.E. Hightower. Frank, you dog!"

I said, "So, that's the reason for all that overtime? Well, that's great, Frank."

"Guys, hold up on the teasing, okay. I don't know how she'd take that. I don't know where this is going to lead."

Clyde summed up our feelings with, "Good for you, Frank. Just enjoy her company for now. Things will work out how things work out."

After Frank left, I looked at Ben, "So, we're going to give them a break on our teasing?"

Ben laughed, "Heck, no. Why should we treat them any differently?"

However, Ben's serious face soon returned, and Clyde and I knew that our large leader was wrestling with a problem: just who would be on the upcoming expedition?

Chapter 9

My kids were leading a charmed life. With numerous 'aunts' and 'uncles' around to spoil them rotten, as the only children in our little neighborhood, they received all sorts of attention. So, when both Marie and I attended the all-hands meeting the next Saturday morning and we brought the kids, they always had someone to play with them. All of the Anchor Farms owners, plus Tom, Diane, and Wheeze, sat around in a circle of lawn chairs to plan our expedition south.

The original Eagles were no longer the tight social group we formed in our youth, but rather a group of business associates. We no longer faced threats of the type that required us to join ranks and fight. Separate occupational, educational, and social interests limited our association to keeping our LLC up and running.

Holden was no longer president Ben, but our chief operating officer. However, while the details of our trip came together, we found ourselves slowly returning to our old militaristic style. During combat training in the military, we all knew the value of a leader because when things got loud and hot, there was always one guy we needed to look to in order to remain organized and effective. There was no time for a committee meeting during a firefight. Ben was gradually assuming his old role.

"Well," Ben began, "it looks like Kelley has gotten us into another mess here."

My sarcastic friends all sighed in unison.

"I've polled all of you and found that eight people want to make this trip, and, due to Wheeze's weight restrictions, only seven can go. Okay, so, Clyde, Dan, Al, Corky, Tom, and I want to go. Wheeze has to go, he's the pilot and mechanic. Another person wants to go," he shot a dirty look toward his wife, "who won't be going, so there's no need for further discussion."

Angie sat fuming.

"However, we now come to Clyde and Corky, and why I'd like to suggest that one of you stay here. You are, without a doubt, the two best wilderness men here, but I'm suggesting one of you remain."

Corky said, "Ben, Clyde and I discussed this earlier, and if one of us has to stay it will be Clyde who goes. He's on the genealogy committee and is a lot closer to Dan. Plus, I think I know why you think this way."

"Yes, I'm a little concerned about this person or persons who created that satellite S.O.S. call. It just worries me, and I would feel better having someone back here who's familiar with firearms and is a good shot. I don't know who or what we are dealing with here. Plus, there's also this Leap Frog company. Frank Davis, you have the scoop on this, right?"

"Yeah. Ms. Hightower and I did some checking on this. Seems they charged three Leap Frog executives with criminal negligence in the drowning deaths of those employees. These executives were never at the site, but were employed by corporations that in turn owned Leap Frog."

"How did it come out?"

"They got off. The flood was considered an act of nature. Then, several civil lawsuits were filed by family members of the drowned employees. It turned into a class action deal. However, the parent companies settled prior to a verdict, the families received money, and I think that was their only concern. A few additional lawsuits were settled over the years, the last one just this month."

"Okay then," Ben went on, "any other business?" Angie raised her hand and our boss reluctantly recognized. "Yes, Mrs. Ben Holden, wife of Ben Holden?"

Angie said, "We still haven't addressed that seventh expedition member."

"We talked about this, Angie, you're not going."

"Why not? Diane Pine went on the last trip and she did fine. What's the matter Bennie, don't want a girl to go?"

"It has nothing to do with that."

"Hey, you guys voted unanimously to allow wives to be full members of Anchor Farms. I was at that meeting. Marie and I do a full share of the work around here and we're just as close to Dan as any of you."

"This isn't an LLC issue, Angie, this is a marital issue. This is between you and me."

"Crapola! Were you serious about this equal partner stuff or did you just do it to make the 'girls' happy?"

"No! It's dangerous out there and I don't want anything to happen to you ... because I love you."

One could hear a pin drop in the room just then.

Angie looked at her husband, and said in a much softer tone, "And just what would my life be without you, Ben? You're all I have. Something could happen to you also. I've been hanging out with you clowns since junior high, and I know the Eagle spirit. I don't mean to be corny here but you guys always said, 'The Eagles fight together or go down together.'"

Corky Wall broke in, "She's right, Ben. She can handle a sidearm better than a lot of us. I know; I taught her. And heck, she is tiny, wouldn't take up much space. We could keep her in the back with the spare tires."

Ben finally conceded, "Okay, I'll go along with this, but I'm not too happy about it. We have seven now. Let's meet again early next week. Bring lists of what we will need to take. Marie, I'd like you to be there. And remember, to anyone outside this room, we're going on our annual late spring hunting and fishing trip. Dan and I will inform Ms. Hightower of our real intentions, but she's the only one."

We then retreated to our garden ground to plant tomatoes. It was an all hands event and we were eager to try out our new system. We hooked up this old flatbed trailer that Milt Frazer gave us behind the tractor. Four people lay on their stomachs facing forward and spaded holes in the ground. Another four lay facing backward and placed tomato plants and pushed back dirt around them. Others walked behind and compacted the soil with their feet. We had to keep the tractor down to a slow crawl, but doing four rows at once made the whole job go much faster.

After lunch, we ran soaker hoses down each row, connected them to our pump, and ran the feed down to the spring south of our garden. Marie insisted that tomatoes preferred spring water over well water.

Marie attended the Saturday night discussion group around the campfire, so I got to watch the kids. While getting stuck with kids' snacks and baths, this also meant that after bedtime I got to lie on the couch. This was just fine with my sore tomato planting muscles.

Centura didn't have much of a downtown, more like a town square. Ben and I walked from the municipal parking lot the next Monday morning over to Ms. Hightower's cramped office suite across the street from the courthouse. Her law firm was growing and she was in need of more space. We brought her a copy of our signed and notarized sharing agreement with Milt Frazer for the loan of his farm equipment.

"These papers seem pretty much in order," she said to us across her desk. While she adjusted her reading glasses, we couldn't help but notice her meticulously managed blonde hair. It was cut very short but always seemed to be perfectly shaped. She could pull it off.

My partner, Ben, was in one of his mischievous moods and I could see he was biting his lip to keep from razzing Ms. H about Frank Davis. On the way up, I asked him to promise me to take it easy on her, but he never did.

"Working a lot of overtime these days?" he asked.

I kicked him in the shin.

"No more than usual," Hightower said, without looking up from the papers.

"I came by late the other night and saw the lights still on. I figured you were practicing a cross-examination."

"Not really."

"Do you examine witnesses the same way over and over, or do you look for different ways?"

Ms. Hightower leaned back in her chair, crossed her arms, and looked at Ben. "Holden, what's the matter with you today?"

"Nothing, just showing an interest in your occupation," Ben said, fighting back the laughter.

Then Ms. H looked at me, "Frank ratted us out, didn't he?" Then she looked up at the clock.

"Great, Ben," I said, "now she's going to bill us for the time you spent teasing her."

She chuckled, "So he told you I could no longer employ him? That I had to fire him?"

"We thought it was because he was a bad kisser," Ben teased.

"No," she said, blushing ever so slightly, "that is certainly not the case. But it does bring up another issue: whether I can represent you guys or not. Frank is a partner in your company. It's a matter of professional ethics."

"How will that work out?" I asked.

"Don't worry. I consulted some other attorneys about it; if I can't represent you I'll set you up with someone good."

"Well," I added, "in spite of the ribbing from my friend here, I want you to know that we're all happy about you and Frank."

"Why, thank you, Dan."

Ben asked, "Can we call you by your first name now?"

"No, you can't. So, guys, I don't think you came up here just to razz me about Frank, and certainly not this sharing agreement you could have emailed. You guys are up to something; I can tell."

"We're going down South again to have a look around," Ben said.

She sighed, "So, what does the military think of this?"

"We aren't going to tell them."

"Why not?"

"We don't trust them. This guy Durham seems sincere, but we've gotten hints that he's keeping an eye on us. He said he wanted to help us, but the only info he's provided is a little blurb on Dan's mom. This seems kind of minimal from a person with his super intelligence gathering methods. I think the government may be behind this whole satellite hacking thing."

Ms. H said, "I disagree. If they didn't want you to know about the hacking, they wouldn't have had that meeting in Captain Richardson's office. In fact, they wouldn't have even mentioned it at all. But here's what I want you to do. I'm going to call in my court reporter and have both of you provide a statement that your main goal on this trip is to help Dan find out about his parents. Don't mention the satellite thing at all. And on your handcomp journals, I want you to keep track of all the things you see and do down there. Okay? Remember guys, national security gives the Federal Government broad powers, so be careful."

As Ben and I walked to his car after we left the building, I said to him, "You don't agree with Hightower, do you?"

"No. I think Patrick O'Dea had some special access to that satellite and I think our Mr. Durham knows all about it."

Since our best cook, Corky Wall, wasn't going, I was charged with getting together the utensils we would need for cooking. Thankfully, the "Beast" meant we didn't have to carry everything in backpacks. There were ten of us on our last trip, and we broke down into two squads of five for cooking purposes. Now with seven, some adjustments had to be made. I decided to forego the tripod, a three-legged cast iron stand that held a pot over a circular campfire, in favor of a 'wreath hanger,' that had four legs supporting a rod running over a rectangular fire. This allowed cooking in several pots at once. For equipment I included a large kettle, some Dutch ovens, a coffee pot, and frying pans. Luckily, Corky had all the cast iron equipment. Each member would have their own mess kit that included two dishes, a coffee cup, and silverware.

Marie made up a list of the food to take. Clyde and Corky were busy drying bison meat and making it into pemmican. We would try to cram in as much as we could because it did not require refrigeration. We would also take some dried beans and pasta. Everything else would have to be hunted or gathered. Plus, I asked Marie to include some serious spices like salt, pepper, garlic, oregano, and cayenne. These would help with those bland roots.

On Wednesday night, the seven voyagers and Marie stood next to the "Beast" in the machine shed while Wheeze gave his tour.

"I had this out and did a couple of laps around the barnyard. I need to do a few more things with the gear ratio to get it right. Now, this thing crawls, about as fast as a brisk walk. I had to gear it down so that it uses less electricity than it produces with the solar cells. On a partly cloudy to fully sunny day, we can run while keeping the batteries fully charged. We can run for a while on a cloudy or rainy day, but more than one in a row and we'll have to sit.

"I'd like two or more people to walk along at all times. In fact, we should have two walking on point to look for debris that might damage a tire. In any case, I don't think you'll like riding inside anyway since there is no air conditioning on this thing. Of course we'll all have to climb on for river crossings. There is room for all of us to sleep in it if we have to. Two in the front seats, Angie crossways behind them, there's two bunks running lengthwise in the back, and two can sleep on the floor in between the bunks.

"On the outside of the driver's side, there is a retractable awning that pulls out when we camp. It's fireproof so we can even build a small fire if it's raining. We do have a drinking and cooking water tank, a microwave, and a small refrigerator. We can draw fresh water with a hand pump when we make stops.

"I'm going to have to bring a couple of spare tires, mounted on top, some tools, grease, lube, and so on. The axles on this are sealed and watertight. It also has a small welder and air compressor built in. We have a great prairie camper here guys."

Ben then said, "So, we all bring our leather backpacks and botas. We won't have to carry water in them, but I want us to have them in case we break down. And a breakdown means we're walking, gang."

"I want everyone to have a sidearm," Clyde said, "everyone that knows how to shoot one of course. I know Dan and Tom don't like them. We'll also have two rechargeable laser weapons for hunting."

"Marie," Ben asked, "how does the food situation look?"

We all returned to our circle of lawn chairs and sat down.

"It looks rather sparse this early. Fishing may be a challenge, the rivers are high. Nuts and berries will almost be nonexistent. There are some greens and early roots. Mushrooms will be plentiful, but let my husband pick those since he knows which ones to get."

Ben concluded, "This weekend we will get all the equipment on the "Beast", and approximate the weight of the food with sandbags. Then we will all go down to the river and see if this baby floats."

I suddenly felt a tug on my shirtsleeve and looked down to see Annie standing there in her pajamas. I looked over to see Diane Pine standing by the door holding Patrick. She shrugged, "She said she just had to talk to you."

I looked down at my daughter, "What's up, honey? Daddy's in a meeting."

"Ice ceam."

Ben Holden responded, "I agree. I say we adjourn to the Kelley house for ice cream."

I led the entourage over to our cabin, Annie held my hand and did her famous ice cream dance when she walked. We then had an impromptu social gathering on our patio while our friends cleaned out our supply of ice cream. Finally, people started to clear out until only the Pines remained.

Marie told the kids, "Okay, brush teeth and then bed."

Diane said to Marie, "I'll go help you. See that look on my husband's face? That's the 'Dan and I need to talk face.' Thank goodness you didn't marry a philosophy major, Marie; they are always coming up with some incredible insight they have to share with someone."

As the four departed to the back bedrooms, I sat next to Tom.

He said, "Well, we have the labor dispute theory, a workplace spat between your dad and Gustav. Then, we have the government conspiracy theory, where Patrick, and possibly his wife, are secret agents running from the DIA. Finally, we have Wheeze's aliens who still live out at Area 51 in the uninhabited desert. Al Myers won't even attempt a guess without more information. What do you think?"

"I honestly don't know, Tom. There are problems with each one of these. Dad worked for Gustav for four or five years. It would have to be a pretty serious spat. Secret agents don't take their little kids out on missions with them. I also don't get the feeling that Durham or Captain Richardson are lying to us. Plus, I don't feel any halfway intelligent alien would want anything to do with this planet. I'm going to have to say none of these, Tom. It's something else."

"Remember when we were down there the last time? Do you remember that sudden windstorm that kicked up? Remember how two independent weathercomps failed to model it? Then, there was that bison herd. You and I, and everyone, knew those bison were headed toward that river north of us to get a drink. However, about a half mile away they made a sudden turn to the east."

"Yeah, and you concluded they picked up our scent."

"How could they do that, Dan? We were north of them! How could they smell us with a forty mile-per-hour wind at their backs? They were avoiding that hill or something between them and that hill. Why would they take a two or three mile detour if it wasn't to their advantage?"

"Are you suggesting some sort of divine or paranormal intervention here?"

"No. I'm just saying that, without some of Al's empirical evidence, the rest of the group has dismissed these details. They are forming beliefs in their own heads and may only accept new evidence that supports those beliefs.

"Dan, I saw something in you when I chose you to become my student. You were just seventeen years old. And that is your ability to accept both the scientific and nonscientific aspects of something before you begin to form an opinion. Yes, you drive people like Al Myers and Dr. Phillips crazy, but that's their problem. You're going to be the only one down on that hill in a few weeks with the right head to get to the bottom of this thing. And you're going to have to take charge down there when we break out with our disagreements, the same arguments we've been having for eight years!"

The next four straight days of continuous rain not only delayed our test float of the "Beast", but also made us realize we were rushing this trip. I recalled from my history studies how both Napoleon and Hitler found themselves overextended in Russia at the wrong time of year. That was winter, of course, but spring can be bad too. It would be a muddy mess down there now and the vegetation not mature. The middle of June would be much better.

During that time, I reread "O'Dea's Riddle," and Living on the Prairie, plus all the comments we received regarding them. I, along with some of the other Eagles, was always under the impression that Patrick and Lilly were either running from something or at something. Our newest clue from the solar panel manual suggested some sort of round trip was in progress. This blew all my theories out of the water. Was Patrick out digging up gold coins at Destinations A, B, C, D and E? Was he under commission to do this for one of the pirates? Was he going to take his share and buy Lilly a new gold watch? Why did he take his family? Why did he leave so late in the season? Destination E was our only hope; whatever was at those first four stops would be there also.

After a few days, however, Ms. Hightower called Ben to inform him that the city council had scheduled a public hearing on their intent to annex our property. The council had not met the required length of time between the notice and the hearing, but Hightower did not intend to make an issue of that since we were prepared.

Centura politics were unique. Since the city was not part of a state, we had no senators or members of the House of Representatives. About seventy years ago, the city petitioned the Federal Government to allow a territorial delegate be elected and sent to Atlanta. However, there was another problem. The current legislation at the time set any uninhabited territorial borders along the lines of the 'Old World' states. Centura city limits were in both Wisconsin and Illinois. So, Congress designated the city a special territorial district. We got our delegate to the House, however, they could only sit on committees and attend sessions; they had no vote, similar to the 'Old World' territories, possessions and commonwealths. What this meant to us was, that to annex current Federal land that Anchor Farms was on, the city council had to have our delegate get one of his congressional friends to write a bill and have it passed into a law. This was such a long and complicated process, Hightower couldn't understand why the city wanted to do it. The Eagles knew why. We saw it similar to the same prejudice against the Southside we experienced in the orphanage.

Ben and I entered a council hearing room that was almost empty. The council was taking their seats and we noticed Ms. Hightower, impeccably dressed and peering into her lapcomp at our table. From her council seat, Betsey Barney saw me walk in but quickly looked away.

The chairperson called the hearing to order, "This is a hearing regarding an ordinance to annex the property on the Southside, submitted by Ms. Barney. Ms. Hightower, who do you represent?"

"Your honor, I represent Anchor Farms Limited Liability Corporation, and its individual partners."

"Proceed with your statement."

"Your honor," she began and walked out into the middle of the floor before the council. "My clients have no objection whatsoever to annexation. This involves no major tax liability to them at all, merely a shift in who they pay. They do, however, own four square miles of land down there, and I noticed that the ordinance only involves their houses. I find this odd."

Gosh, I loved watching this woman in a hearing. She looked at the council members straight in the eye, did not read from notes when she spoke, and maintained an air of total confidence.

The council chair asked, "Are these residences up to code?"

"Yes, your honor, all work was done by competent parties. Electrical work was done by a licensed electrician, Mr. Kelley here. In fact my clients, at their own expense, hired a city inspector who found everything in order. Their concern is regarding city services."

"How do they handle their trash now?"

"They haul it themselves to the city landfill and pay a nonresident fee to dump it. A fee, your honor, which is more than they would pay if they were annexed residents."

"Then, what is their concern?"

Ms. Hightower then began pacing back and forth in front of the entire length of the council table, looking up at them at certain times. "There is nothing in this ordinance describing the city's intent in providing these services. There is no funding allocation or timetable for constructing sewer lines. Where is the money coming from?"

"The city will do that if this ordinance is passed."

"Will they, your honor?"

"Please be a little more frank, Ms. Hightower," the chair was becoming frustrated.

"Come on, your honor, isn't this the old Southside shuffle? We all know how that works. South Shore Drive was resurfaced ten years ago, and North Shore Drive was done five years ago. Guess which road got resurfaced just this last fall? You added three new staff to the Northside museum this year, yet you cut four from the orphanage on the Southside."

"We annexed that log home division just east of Anchor Farms and had those sewer lines and streets done within six months."

"And that annexation request sat on your desk for two years, and it didn't pass until all those rich people started moving down there."

"Do you have any additional pertinent information to add, Ms. Hightower?"

"That concludes my statement, your honor." She returned to her seat next to Ben and whispered to him, "Darn, I blew that one. I came on too strong."

Ben whispered back, "Don't worry. This issue was decided long before the meeting started."

The chair addressed the council, "I move we add this ordinance to the agenda of our next formal meeting for a vote. All those in favor, raise their right hand." We saw two members to the left of the chair raise their hands. We were stunned to see no hands go up on the right, including Ms. Barney.

The chair was about to hit her gavel when she stopped in midair and turned toward Betsey, "Ms. Barney, you were the one who submitted this ordinance."

"I know. I would like to withdraw it until I can obtain a budget and timetable from city operations."

"Well," the chair concluded, "the motion fails. This hearing is adjourned." She pounded the gavel hard.

Ben and I turned to Ms. Hightower who was still stunned from the verdict. "What the heck just happened here?"

Ben said, "This whole thing is old stuff, Ms. H. This is something between Barney and us that goes back to junior high school. We can become professionals, add value to the city, get married, have kids, get PhDs. and write books, but we'll always be those orphans on the Southside. Now Barney had some sort of burst of good conscience here, but I'm sure it's an aberration."

"Well, her 'burst' was certainly timely," our attorney said while she stuffed her lapcomp into her brief case. "But of course you'll get my bill anyway. And Holden, can you pay me before the next ice age this time?"

Bright sunshine returned the next Saturday, while Wheeze, on our tractor, pulled the 'Beast' along on the trailer and the rest of us followed in my pickup truck. We took the main road that led to town and then turned left where the James River passed through Milt's field.

After he stopped, Wheeze pulled the 'Beast' off of the trailer. We had a short christening ceremony with Annie touching the bottle to the side of our vehicle, but Marie took over to actually break it. We didn't have any champagne so we used a bottle of Corky's homemade barbecue sauce.

Wheeze yelled, "Boaaarrd!"

The seven of us climbed in and on. I rode on top to check the connectivity of the solar modules while we were underway. The 'Beast' did quite well on land, moving steadily, and seemed to have sufficient power. Things got a little tense when Wheeze pulled up to the river and prepared to sail.

Marie ran up to the side of the vehicle and yelled, "Dan, you keep your life insurance policy in your desk, right?"

"Yeah, 'Mrs. Confidence', and Hightower has a copy. Spend the money wisely, honey. I love you, too."

Clyde had supplied the 'Beast' with inflatable life jackets, just in case. We all put them on while Wheeze entered the water and turned on the propellers. While crossing the current, the thing tossed and turned a bit, but going straight up and down the river was smooth. Plus it even went a little faster in the water than on land. While I wouldn't want to cross the Atlantic in it, I felt pretty safe and folks in the cabin reported no leaks.

At the Saturday night cookout, Wheeze was ecstatic, "That thing is so cool. It's like having an RV and a boat in one. When can we leave?"

"Ben suggested June 17th, at 4:00 a.m., weather permitting," Clyde indicated. "I tend to agree. The rivers may be down then and the prairie much drier."

Wheeze went on, "Okay. I can use the time to train some other drivers, but we can do that around the barnyard. I'll do the river crossings, but I can't see why some others couldn't drive on land. The thing crawls along. We just have to be careful not to drive over any rubble."

"I think we will be fine," Clyde said. "Those are some 'beefy boy' tires."

"The hull is a titanium alloy, super-strong but super-lightweight. As long as that thing sat out in the weather down there, I saw no deterioration of the metal whatsoever. I think it's our best defense against the aliens. What do you think, Kelley?"

I laughed. "Wheeze, why don't you ask Al? He loves questions like that."

"Hey, Dr. Al," Wheeze yelled across the fire, "do you think that titanium hull will stop an alien 'ray gun'?"

"Heck, yeah. I have an experimental 'ray gun' in the machine shed. Why don't you sit in the 'Beast' and we'll see."

We dined on Angie's special vegetable au gratin that was quite tasty. However, some of us snuck a strip or two of bison jerky in our shirt pockets and bit off pieces when she wasn't looking.

Ben called another impromptu meeting after we finished cleaning up. "Okay, I have good news. Our friends up at Thompson are going to be starting their annual war games north of the base on the eighteenth. That means a lot of men and equipment will be involved. I hear also that Captain Richardson will be taking some ships up there also. This means they will be distracted and have less time to worry about what we're up to. After we get about twenty or thirty miles away, our handcomp and quantanet connections will drop off. About ten miles out, we'll all switch them over to our server here where calls will be switched to a recorded message saying we're out in the woods hunting and fishing. Corky will review them daily and determine if anything needs his attention. Also, load up your handcomp memories with anything you'll need on the trip like recipes, 'Old World' maps, first aid procedures, and so on. Al will have all the 'Destination E' files on his.

"I've asked Frank Davis to be acting manager in my absence. He'll need something to distract him from Ms. Hightower. Frank also has an announcement to make."

"Yes. I guess some of you have guessed that I have moved back here permanently."

Some of us 'booed'.

"Yesterday I got accepted to the faculty at the law school and this fall will be teaching financial law. I want to thank everyone for helping me return to single life and welcoming me back home. I should have never left; you guys are my family."

We all clapped.

"Okay," Ben said, "those of you who are going, get your affairs in order. We leave on the seventeenth."

Chapter 10

I was sure it was the urge for discovery that woke me up at 2:30 on the morning of June 17th, but with the first few sips of coffee 'those' nagging doubts started to enter my mind. Would I be able to withstand another big letdown on that hill? I knew all my friends were anxious to go on a camping trip; I never doubted their support. But how much longer could I keep their interest up? I was experiencing what Tom Pine described as an approach/avoidance conflict. I wanted to find out more, but wasn't sure of the consequences of total failure.

After I enjoyed my last hot shower for what could be several weeks, I dressed in my army fatigues and stuffed a change of clothes in my backpack. I placed it on the counter alongside the expedition's precious coffee supply.

Our bedroom was still completely dark, but I saw Marie sitting up in bed. I said, "I tried to explain to the kids last night that I would be gone for a while. Patrick was oblivious and I don't think Annie understood. She thinks I'm just going to work."

"Look under your pillow."

I reached in and pulled out a little wallet-sized picture of the two kids at Christmas.

"She didn't want you to forget what they looked like."

"Little chance of that," I said and then hugged and kissed her.

"Be careful and stay out of trouble."

I laughed, "I'm sure all incidents of bad behavior will be reported to you by Angie."

As I made my way to the machine shed, the only sounds being made were two crickets who didn't know it was past bedtime. The sky was jet black, no stars, and just a slight breeze.

Ben, Angie, and Wheeze were already there. Angie was brushing her long, black hair and looked like she was ready to go to sleep while standing up.

Ben informed Wheeze, "We'll be making a tight circle around Old Chicago to avoid the rubble piles. Once on the other side, we'll then take a course due south. The rivers are smaller going this way and easier to cross."

"Rivers shouldn't be a problem at all with this baby taking us across."

I secured two of my favorite throwing staffs, the throwing spears I took into the wilderness as a kid, to the top of the 'Beast' while Al, Tom, and Clyde entered. Everyone knew the drill and how to dress for the occasion. Good watertight combat boots and clothes of sturdy fabric were a must. Clyde went over a checklist to be sure we had all the required equipment. Everyone made sure I stored the coffee in one of the airtight containers in the back of the vehicle.

Ben then gave his pep talk, and lightened the mood a little, "Okay guys, everyone please remember to stuff wrappers and other trash in your pockets and then throw them in the campfire every evening. No need to mess up the land the good Lord took one thousand years to clean up. Let's do our assigned jobs, work hard, and all that Lewis and Clark type-stuff. But let's have some fun too; we haven't been on an expedition this far out in years."

So exactly at 4:00 a.m. we headed out. Clyde and I walked point and Ben walked along next to the driver's door. We went straight south for two miles, to the end of our property, and then due west along our southern border with the uninhabited land. After getting to our winter caves, we kept west out into several miles of rolling hills and low brush. The sun slowly began to rise, and I hopped on the 'Beast' while Angie relieved me walking point with Clyde. Hiking was much easier this time due to being able to throw our packs and weapons on the vehicle instead of lugging them around.

Once the terrain became more open prairie, Ben hopped on and sat next to me on top. The 'Beast' performed well. Cruising along at 3.1 miles per hour, the only sounds we heard were small fallen branches being crunched under the wheels. We could easily hear the conversation Clyde and Angie were having out on point.

"You seem rather quiet today, Clyde, everything okay?" Angie asked.

"I have some issues."

"Want to talk about them?"

"No thanks. They're my problems."

Ben elbowed me.

Early morning turned to midmorning that turned to early afternoon. We didn't stop for lunch; rather we munched on jerky and some homemade bread that Angie brought. We continued to rotate our walks on point.

In the afternoon, I sat shotgun while Angie poked her head up between the seats. She asked, "Wheeze, do you consider yourself a Goth?"

He laughed and said, "I guess so. I guess college boy Kelley here would say I have Goth tendencies."

"Why the black clothes and tattoos?"

"I think it had to do with our moods. I mean, I guess I was kind of a melancholy kid. I had no mom, and my Dad was in and out of prison when I was growing up. A few of us wore black as a social statement, a show of disapproval about the way things were. There were a lot of groups like that in history, Kelley can tell you. Beatniks, Hippies, and Goths were just a few. How we dressed was how we recognized each other."

"Weren't they also linked to being violent?"

"Do you know what my friends and I did, Angie? We worked on cars, listened to music, and talked about tattoos. We kept to ourselves and didn't bother anybody. It wasn't until violent people came walking around in our neighborhood that we got violent. They would yell at us, 'Hey, we don't like that music; turn it off.' Now, we didn't care what music they listened to, but nobody comes in my garage or my house and turns my music off. I guess when you dress weird you attract attention. I was too violent at times, for sure, and I know now it's not the way to handle things.

"I don't know where this gang name, The Range, came from. There was no The Range before the Mustangs. No, we weren't naturally violent, the violence came to us. The same thing happened with Kelley and the Eagles. They became Eagles-the-gang after the Musties took a few shots at them. It was like a scene I think. Kelley, what's the right word here?"

"Setting, forum, venue, or arena. Everyone was saying we were on our own, and it was the only way we knew."

Angie changed the subject, "Hey, either of you know what's up with Clyde? He's acting funny."

Wheeze said, "Not really."

I said, "No."

We stopped to camp about 3:00 p.m. that day and Wheeze made sure he parked on the west side of a tree grove to keep sunlight on the solar cells as long as possible. He pulled out the awning while Angie and I set up to cook. Ben had suggested, instead of hunting or fishing, we use some of the pemmican to reduce the weight of the 'Beast'. The others walked through the tree grove to check for predators.

"I hate to bring this up," Angie said, "but what do we do about bathroom needs?"

Wheeze handed her a shovel and this little milking stool with a hole in the seat. "Dig a hole, place the stool over it, then cover."

Angie made a face, "Did we think to bring any toilet paper?"

"Leaves," Wheeze said, "Be sure to find some smooth ones."

"Yuck. I should have listened to my husband about making this trip."

After I obtained some roots and wild mushrooms and washed them in a brook, I put a kettle of pemmican ragout on a slow fire. Our camp routine came back to us quickly. Stones to encircle the fire and dried fallen branches were gathered. We set up our sleeping bags in a semicircle facing the fire, using the hull or tires of the 'Beast' for back supports.

Although we had a huge kettle, we ate every bit of that stew. Luckily, we had some of Angie's bread left over. However, breakfast was going to take even more stored supplies. Our female travel mate and resident vegetarian decided to suspend her no-meat diet for the rest of the trip.

After cleanup, we told stories of our previous trip. We quieted around sunset because some of the guys had to get to sleep, especially the ones who had to stand their two-hour watch at times during the night.

Angie relieved Clyde on watch at 10:00 p.m. She walked out to meet him while he was encircling the camp. "You're off, bud, sweet dreams."

"Thanks," Clyde said.

"Feel like talking yet?"

"No, it's kind of personal. You know, the other guys will never let me hear the end of it."

"Clyde, you can always talk to me. I'll keep it confidential."

"Let me think about it. Maybe a woman's opinion will help."

Al Myers woke me from a deep sleep at four in the morning. Surprisingly, I was usually awake on my own at this time, but I guess I needed to build up my hiking stamina. Al flopped down on his sleeping bag, and I fed the fire and put on the coffee pot.

I walked in a tight circle around our camp during my watch, lugging one of the laser weapons. All was dead quiet. Tree groves were packed close together this far north, the surrounding ones less than a hundred or so yards away. I scanned the edges of these groves while I walked, keeping an eye out for predatory animals.

I thought of Wheeze's discussion of yesterday, and how predatory humans were much more stupid than their animal counterparts. The Mustangs had not respected their victims. Their carnivore animal counterparts did. Predatory animals studied their potential meals. I could see this in the eyes of the alpha wolf that threatened us on our earlier trip. Even the fiercest predators expected their victims to defend themselves.

There would be fights and casualties. There were no 'protected rights guaranteed by the Constitution'; this was king-of-the-jungle type-stuff. Of advantage to our four-legged counterparts was that they were all aware of this. It was the law out here, and the animals knew this going in.

When the sky in the east began to lighten up, I woke the others. We went through two dozen eggs for breakfast. Ben thought we should empty our little fridge as soon as possible so we could utilize it to store meat. With only eight dozen eggs stuffed in there, this would not take long.

After the sun cleared the horizon, we were on our way again. Tom Pine and I rode together on the roof of the 'Beast'.

"I've been meaning to ask you," he said. "How did you score Dr. Phillips' prize electric motor?"

"Oh, that. I just did what you taught me to do: transactional analysis."

"How so?"

"Consider his statement of 'I want you in electrical engineering.' At first, I was considering the wrong part of his sentence. I began to realize it was never about my future or his love of his field. It was the 'I want' part. He wanted to increase his student count; he wanted the straight 'A' boy in his program. So I just gave him what he wanted; I enrolled."

"But he disapproved your request. Why?"

"Because his love for his occupation suddenly returned, or he figured out what I was doing. I was acting just like him. I think he saw that. He's not stupid."

Tom said, "Isn't it interesting how the 'I want' is becoming the most important part of almost everyone's statements these days? It's the default. I think sometimes if people didn't need an audience to communicate their desires, they wouldn't talk to anyone else at all. If someone ever came in and asked me, 'Tom, how can I make your life easier today?' I would jump right out my office window."

Tom and I walked point together after that. Later that morning, we ran into a rough stretch of ground that caused us to take extra care in watching where we stepped.

Clyde took over driving the 'Beast' that afternoon, but, around 2:30, he brought it to a stop on a small hill next to the most gorgeous lake I had ever seen. Dark clouds in the west led to the decision to stop early and get camp going before the rain hit. I wanted to go fishing but was tagged by Ben to dig out a water trench. With our little army shovels, we made a trench, about six inches deep, all around the 'Beast' and in front of the awning. We then dug some channels down all sides of the hill to run rainwater off and away from camp.

Clyde and Wheeze got lucky fishing and came back with walleye nearly as long as Angie. The three of them, after cleaning them, got out frying pans and started cooking up fish. We ate in shifts, after each batch got done, for over two hours. I think I had three courses.

Just when the last person took the last bite, the wind picked up and caused us to scramble to clean and store equipment. The awning was not going to be much protection against windblown rain, and we all retreated into the vehicle.

The 'Beast' was crowded and the air foul, but it sure beat sleeping in one of those two-man pup tents we used on the last trip. Soon a deck of cards appeared and most of us were engaged in games of five-card draw.

"I can't believe how much I ate," Angie said, holding her stomach.

Clyde said, "We experienced this on the last trip. You're working muscles you don't use that much and you are burning more calories. After a few days, it will even out. I think you'll find that you'll be fitter when you get back; it's all this exercise and fresh air."

"Well, the air in here sure isn't fresh," she added, "When is bath day?" Angie had her hair up in a bun and was trying to secure it.

"Grab a bar of soap and have a natural shower," her husband said.

"Right. I think a shower in this would be a tad cold."

This was a night I didn't have a watch, and was certainly thankful. We could at least walk around outside, but sitting in this stuffy cabin and trying to stay awake for two hours proved difficult for the watch standers.

I opened my eyes and saw that it was around eight in the morning. Just about to jump up, I heard the rain hitting the roof of the 'Beast' and figured we were in a weather delay.

Then I heard Angie's voice, "Gosh, does it ever stink in here."

"We have 'odeur-de-prairie'," Ben said.

"Did you guys know you snore in unison?" she went on. "You sound like a poorly-tuned brass section in a marching band."

Wheeze asked, "What's for breakfast?"

I answered, "Reheated fish. I'll start the coffee."

Getting up from the floor, I exited through one of the hatches in the roof. Outside I found our wet stack of firewood and it took me a while to get a fire going. I finally got the coffee on while everyone else came outside.

The rain only lasted until midmorning when the clouds cleared and the sun came out. I was hoping we would get going by noon, but Ben suggested we take a day off, let the land dry out, and utilize this great lake for baths and clothes washing. The 'Beast' was a blessing of sorts, but also a curse. We could have easily gotten in ten miles by nightfall, if we were on foot.

Our vehicle was performing above expectations. We used very little power overnight because we did most tasks outside. The batteries were never below ninety-four percent charged. Wheeze was still reluctant to try running in total overcast or after sundown because he always wanted some power in reserve. In any event, everyone was having such a good time on this trip that no one objected to a few extra days.

Although I was a little frustrated regarding the delay, we did have a good time that afternoon. We took baths and washed clothes at the same time. Ben escorted Angie to a private inlet of the lake for their hygiene activities. Later, I got to fish and pulled in more than we could eat. In the later afternoon, we sat around the fire and wrote in our ejournals.

The GPS function on our handcomps still worked out here because the satellites transmitted these data nationwide. However, general quantanet access wasn't available; it required a relay tower because of all that decoding and unscrambling equipment owned by the military.

Ben and Wheeze took a turn at cooking that evening and we had fish again. The ground dried up enough to sleep on so we laid out our sleeping bags around the fire.

I was awakened around midnight by a poke in my back. I heard many of the guys rustling in their sleeping bags. Clyde was up to take over watch from Angie. The two whispered and walked around to the front of the 'Beast'.

"What's up?" Angie asked in a hushed voice.

Clyde said, "This is just too much for me. I don't know how to handle this."

"Clyde, take it easy. It can't be that bad. You have a lot of friends here."

"That's my problem. I'm sort of obsessed with another woman. Angie, I'm having an 'affair'."

"You're cheating on Mary?"

"No, it's more just a mental thing right now, but it could turn bad in an instant."

"Oh, Clyde, you have to get this out of your mind, or at least be up front with Mary. Just get over it. Does the other woman know it?"

"I think so."

"Well, tell her it's over for crying out loud. Do I know her?"

"Yes. And to make it worse, she's married to a friend of mine."

Angie paused, then, "Holy cow, it's not Marie Kelley is it? That would just kill Dan."

"No, it's not her."

"Who?"

"Angie, I'm totally and madly in love with you. I can't help myself."

We heard this shrill scream in the night and Angie yelling at the top of her voice, "Oh, gag me with a fork, Clyde!" Our little friend came storming back into camp to see all of us sitting up in our sleeping bags laughing our heads off. Ben was laughing so hard he was holding his sides.

"Are you in on this?" She kicked her husband hard in the leg. It looked like it hurt but it didn't stop Ben from laughing.

Clyde walked up, "You guys should have seen the look on her face."

"You think this is funny?" Angie yelled at Ben. "Well, you'll think it's real funny when you get a big, fat divorce notice in the mailbox when we get back!" She started to climb up the ladder into the vehicle, "I'm going to sleep in the 'Beast'; I don't have to take this crap off you guys."

We all sat and laughed. Then Clyde knocked on the window and said, "Angie, don't fight it. I've seen that look on your face too."

We heard a muffled voice from inside, "Yeah, that's the face I get right before I throw up!"

Ben poked me again, but this time it was four in the morning and time for my watch.

My lookout was uneventful save for around five when I noticed some rustling in the bushes about a hundred yards from camp. I threw a few more branches on the fire and kept my eye on it, but after a while whatever it was left.

When I got back to the fire, Angie was getting the frying pans out and greasing them up. I knelt down beside her, "I love you too, Angie."

"Yeah, let's see if you love me after I whack you in the head with this frying pan a couple of times." Then a smile broke out on her face, "Ya know, it's a good thing you guys got Clyde to do that. You or Tom could never have pulled it off; I would never have believed you."

We were on the move at seven. After only a few miles, a big clear sky broke out. The tree groves thinned out from every few hundred yards to every two or three miles. Clyde and I walked point and were in awe of the grand view, stretching to the horizon. The grass was still bright green from spring rains; wildflowers bloomed everywhere.

Clyde slung his weapon over his shoulder, put both arms straight up in the air, and yelled, "This is what I'm talkin' about!"

We decided to go until 4:00 p.m. since we didn't need to take time to hunt. We soon doubted this decision after we climbed to the top of a large hill only to see the Illinois River before us on the other side. Wheeze stopped the 'Beast' and we all got out, and stood and gazed at it.

"Holy cow," Angie gasped, "that sure is one big river. I thought we took this more eastern route to avoid big rivers."

"It must be up from heavy rains," Clyde said while he looked through his field glasses. "That's at least a half mile across. I had hoped our first river crossing would be shorter."

"Maybe we should do it in the morning," Al Myers suggested.

Clyde said, "It's always better to cross a river just before we camp. It could be even higher if we get rain tonight."

"Anything we can dump to lighten the load?" a nervous Tom Pine asked.

Wheeze said, "Nothing that's going to make much difference. Come on guys, we can do it. Eagles never say die."

We all donned our life preservers and Ben went over how they worked. They contained a small canister of compressed gas that inflated the vests with a pull on a cord.

Wheeze wanted two spotters on top and, since everyone mistakenly assumed I had some special knowledge gained from the Navy, I was elected. I sat on the front with Ben on the rear. Even though our macho pride kept us from mentioning it, I was pretty sure we were all anxious.

Wheeze took the 'Beast' into the water at a slow crawl. After drifting out a few feet, he started the propellers. I had to cling to an equipment mount while we gained speed, but then the ride smoothed out. Ben and I kept an eye out for floating tree limbs.

Our tattooed helmsman seemed to display his weird sense of humor at the most anxious times. Apparently, he rolled his window down and sat up on the windowsill, sticking his head over the roof. "Arrrgh, matie. Go splay the jib and be ye quick about it."

I responded, "I don't know how to 'splay' anything."

"Well then, go shiver me timbers. Heck, you were in the Navy; go do something sailor-like. Hey, Kelley, look," he held both arms up in the air. "I'm steering this 'Beast' with my feet."

I laughed, but big Ben didn't think much of it, "Wheeze, get back inside and steer it right or you'll be sleeping with the fishes!"

"Aye, aye, Cap'n." Wheeze disappeared below decks.

We approached the middle of the river, and the current picked up and suddenly pitched the 'Beast' into a forty-five degree roll. Spray kicked up from the front and drenched Ben and I. Wheeze handled it well by swiftly turning downstream. This way he wouldn't be fighting the current and we could inch over to the south while we went. Of course, this made the trip over that much longer and put us about two miles off course to the west.

After getting into calmer waters near shore, Wheeze picked out a long sloping bank to beach the craft. He pulled up, once again on wheel power, and stopped up on the grass.

Apparently, the cabin crew did not enjoy the trip. Angie got out, knelt down and pretended to be praying, and Al kissed the ground.

We looked up to see Wheeze, with one hand on his hip and the other pointing off into the distance. "Arrrgh. I do hereby claim this land in the name of Queen Isabella of Spain. And I - dub thee the Commonweal of the Spanish Indies."

Angie laughed, "Hey, Columbus, this is Illinois, blockhead."

"Oh, so it is. Well, I'm sure Izzy will like Illinois, too. Even though that's French."

Joking aside, after the anxiety of the crossing faded away, I noticed a return of our good natures. Sometimes it takes a little tension to get our blood pumping. We sang pirate songs around the campfire that evening.

I also noticed the group's good mood the next day. Wheeze let me drive the 'Beast' and most of the others walked alongside. I noticed a little extra spring in our steps, and the jokes continued all day. Angie promised Clyde she was going to poison his food for pulling that stunt on her.

Keeping track of all our jokes in his ejournal, Tom Pine vowed his next book was going to be about this trip with a mixture of philosophy and humor.

Life was, indeed, different out here. There were no committee meetings, research papers, or tax forms. Robert's Rules of Order, Modern Language Association documentation style, or double entry bookkeeping didn't apply. All restraints of civilization faded away. Lesser used senses became more active. The sounds and scents of nature were parts of an experience that civilized humans have forgotten about. In a way, there was a certain 'carefreeness' about it. We decided the route to take;

we decided which tree grove to explore. We didn't need permission.

We stopped about three in the afternoon that day because we wanted to stock up on our food supply. Wheeze pulled into a grove of trees next to a shallow stream.

Clyde and Angie went out to hunt and returned with pheasants while the rest of us set up camp. We hung the birds over a slow fire. This was by far the most pleasant setting we had camped in to date. I sat on my sleeping bag and updated my ejournal when Tom sat down beside me.

"Won't be long now," Tom said.

"Al thinks we're only a day and a half away."

"Any more insightful ideas?"

I laughed, "Not a one. The journey so far has been such a blast, I'm not sure I've even thought much about the destination. Maybe going there with an open mind is best."

"How about ..."

Tom stopped midsentence, when suddenly Wheeze came running out of the trees at sprint speed. Right behind him were five gray wolves, and they were running just as fast. When Wheeze hit the streambed, water flew out from beneath his feet.

Before we could move, Clyde drew his pistol while he squatted down and, holding it with both hands, fired a shot. A tip of an ear and blood from the lead wolf flew up in the air, causing the animal to tumble head over heels. Howling in pain, he stood up and retreated back into the trees, while the rest followed him.

Wheeze got to the bank near us and turned to see them running off. "Did you miss?"

"No," Clyde said, "I just wanted to graze an ear and send him running. It'll heal."

Wheeze gasped, "That was a twenty or thirty yard shot. You were aiming for his ear?"

"I'm awful good with this gun," Clyde smiled, putting the pistol back in the arm holster. "Did you stumble into them?"

"Yeah. I think they were just waking up. I didn't even have time to draw my gun."

"Okay. They won't be back. I just wanted to 'wing' the leader. If he turns and runs, the rest will follow. It was better not to kill him, since he knows now not to mess with us. We'll be okay."

Clyde's reassurance did little to calm my nerves. I kept one eye on those trees the rest of our time there.

I did find plenty of mushrooms and tender roots, and Angie fried them up in a great sauce. The meal was the best we had had since leaving Centura.

Before turning in, Clyde and I walked the tree grove one more time, if only to calm my nerves. We saw that the wolves had left the area.

Being assigned the 4:00 a.m. watch suited me just fine. I got the fire blazing and put on the coffee. My friends appeared to know I was anxious to get on the trail, so they were all up early getting breakfast ready. We took off about six.

Our present route merged with the route we took down here eight years ago, and I began to recognize landmarks here and there. I was so much in a hurry to get there, when walking point I actually started to outwalk the 'Beast'. Ben had to yell at me to slow me down.

After a short detour around a rubble hill, I could see the tree line along the river where we camped out eight years ago.

However, on the open prairie, objects appeared closer than they actually were. It seemed like it took forever to get there, but we finally arrived around one in the afternoon.

Just like the last time here, we found the banks of this river to be steep. We decided to get out and let Wheeze cross it without the extra weight. Getting up the far bank required him to engage the six-wheel drive. The rest of us crossed, hand over hand, on a rope. Wheeze then turned the vehicle around pointing east so our camp could face the river.

I ran to the 'Beast' and stood on top. Through the field glasses, about a mile and a half away, I saw our prize. The three oak trees still stood there, alone on the hill.

Tom stood on the ground and looked up at me, "Still there?"

"Still there," I said excitedly. "One of the oaks has a limb down. It was probably a lightning strike. Tell Wheeze I don't see any space ships parked there."

I wanted to do nothing more than grab a weapon and take a hike over there, but I knew Ben would raise heck if I tried. I knew the drill. Our leader wanted us to refill our water, get some food cooked, wash clothes and bathe before heading over there in the morning. I guess I could last another few hours, but no more.

We spent the rest of the afternoon doing those things. Tom suggested we also tie some extra firewood on top of the 'Beast' because there was certainly not any up on that hill.

Clyde and Ben went hunting and this time returned with some venison steaks. What we didn't eat that night we stuck in our refrigerator for use on the hill.

Angie insisted on taking my 10:00 p.m. watch that night. Although I thought I would be too nervous to sleep, it must have been the effects of too much adrenaline that day because I fell into a sound sleep and slept all night.

Wheeze woke me at six thirty and I saw they had most of the camp packed up by then. I only had time for a cup of coffee.

Retrieving one of my staffs from atop the 'Beast', I started walking south. I was taking point and no one tried to argue with me.

Chapter 11

I approached the hill with at least a one hundred yard lead on the rest of the expedition. However, Clyde Hastings, with a laser weapon, was walking out in front of the 'Beast,' keeping an eye on me. "The hill" as we called it, was only a gradual rise, a high spot of not more than a couple of acres, on the endless prairie. The three oak trees, slowly waving in a slight breeze, stood sentinel at the highest point. I walked among them and stopped to look around.

I knew this place well. The three- or four-inch prairie grass was a brighter green than on my last visit, but little else was different. One of the oaks had dropped a high branch. The charred end told me it was from a lightning strike, and its dried out appearance indicated it fell over a year ago. Nevertheless, everything else was exactly the same as I remembered it on our last visit here eight years ago. Sometimes, I think I had never left.

Something was missing though. I recalled how we felt marching toward this spot the first time and how I was anticipating the solution to a great mystery, how something magical would happen as soon as I stood on the summit. But today that feeling was elusive. There were three oak trees and some grass; there was nothing else here. There was no mysterious strong wind.

However, I knew more about things now than I had eight years ago. This was 'Destination E'; my father wrote down the GPS coordinates to this spot. He was coming here, just like he did 'Destinations A' through 'D'. What he found at those previous spots was here also. I said aloud, "It's here."

"Great, Dan," I was startled by Clyde standing right behind me, "you only been here for five minutes and you're already talking to yourself."

Wheeze, driving the 'Beast', was following close behind. He pulled around and pointed the vehicle north, to give us a western-facing campsite. All of the 'troops' got out and started setting up camp.

Angie was unimpressed. She put her hands on her hips and looked around, "This is the place you guys have been yapping about for the last ten years? I expected to see a fountain or a statue of the Mona Lisa or something."

"It's here," Tom Pine told her, then looked at me and winked, "we just have to find it."

Clyde got a small fire going and Ben, knowing it was going to be a long day, started to brew a pot of coffee. Wheeze and I got some poles and canvas out of the 'Beast' and erected a small teepee to the south of the campsite for our toilet facilities. There were no bushes to hide behind for miles.

After Wheeze was handed the shovel, he looked over at our leader and said, "Hey Ben."

"What?"

"I disagree with the job assignments. I'm the mechanical genius behind this expedition and you got me digging the latrine."

We all laughed while Ben replied, "It will be good practice for when your wife makes you sleep in the backyard."

After setup was complete, Clyde walked out about two hundred feet and slowly patrolled the perimeter. He looked down at the ground and then out to the horizon in each direction.

Al Myers walked around, repeating all the tests he had on our last trip. He took soil samples, samples from the oaks, and repeated the ground penetrating radar readings of the ground beneath. He checked something; I didn't understand what, with the magnetic fields. He repeated his tests of the air and moisture content of the soil.

After about an hour, a frustrated Dr. Myers looked up at me, "This is crap, Dan! Everything's the same. Everything is just like it was eight years ago. I don't know what I expected to find here and why I even came on this trip."

"Dr. Myers, what is it you are a doctor of, anyway?" Wheeze asked.

"Theoretical mathematics."

"What do they do?"

"Lots of things. I work with imaginary numbers."

"What are those?"

"Well, like the square root of a negative number. They do have some uses."

"Like what?"

"Well, they make certain equations work out."

"I figure an equation like that is one I should stay away from."

Tom Pine interrupted, "What's your point, Wheeze?"

"Well, we have a philosopher and a math guy here, I'm just wondering how we're going to solve this situation."

"Well, Al knows the principles behind scientific inquiry, so we need him."

Al said, "I just wish those principles would help me out more right now."

Ben, sensing the dejection of our science officer, called us over to the fire for a meeting. He served each of us a brunch of jerky strips and the last of our eggs. While we ate, he said, "Let's go around and get your thoughts. Al, you start."

"Oh, Ben, you know I hate doing this without empirical data. I don't know. I don't know. I don't know!"

"A guess is all I'm asking for, an opinion."

"I don't have enough information."

"None of us have enough information, Al," Tom said.

"Oh, I don't know. Please don't take offense, Dan, but the pirate motivation seems to be the most likely. I think Patrick may have been looking for treasure. I know, I've not discovered any treasure and I can't explain that satellite hacking thing."

"I'm still with the thought that Patrick was working for or against the government" Ben said. "I believe he was on the run. He did have the 'Beast', a military vehicle, and only someone in the government could have hacked that satellite."

Ben looked at Angie and Clyde but neither had a guess.

Wheeze added, "I'm still going with the aliens, although I'm not going to rule out zombies." We all laughed but he went on, "I don't mean to joke about this stuff, but you guys have to admit there was something unworldly going on here. Oh, what's the word ...?"

"Paranormal," Tom said.

"Right, that stuff."

Tom Pine said, "I'm a philosopher, a romantic if you will. I see things, not so much as scientific, but as motivations, desires, qualities, and so on. I'm not an expert in this scientific

178

stuff, but we're dealing with magnetic forces and math equations. We need to look higher."

"A divine answer?" Clyde asked.

"Maybe 'higher' is not the right word; maybe it's lower, but in any event, deeper. We need to delve into Patrick's motivations on some kind of level that we're overlooking with our equations and gadgets. It's like Clyde knowing about the behavior of wolves. It's here, I know it. And it's something so incredibly obvious, we can't see it."

Our meeting ended then. I wasn't asked my opinion, but then, I knew why. I didn't have one yet, although everyone was looking at me to provide the solution. I had some good guesses about the middle of my Dad and Mom's journey, but I was missing the important parts. It was like reading the middle two-thirds of a novel; I had no beginning or end. I slowly walked around the site, for over an hour, and pondered.

Clyde returned to his walk around the perimeter. After a while, I noticed him spending a long time looking east with his field glasses. For a diversion, I walked out to him.

"See something?"

He spoke without taking his eyes out of the binoculars, "No, not really." He was fixed on a line of trees, about a mile or so in the distance. "I see nothing, and that's what is bothering me."

After I returned to walk among the three oaks, I almost wanted to ask those trees what was here. For fear of being hospitalized along with Bo Schlitz, I remained quiet.

After a while, Angie walked over to me with a cup of coffee. "There's smoke coming out of your ears, Danny boy. Here, drink this."

"Thanks, Shorty."

We laughed, and then engaged in some small talk.

"So what do you think Marie and the kids are up to?" Angie asked.

"Marie's probably cursing me because we're not around to take care of the garden. Annie's probably asking for me, but only because she knows I'll give in and get her some ice cream."

"Those kids are growing like weeds."

"Wait, I have a picture here." I reached into the inside pocket of my army shirt, where I keep my handcomp, and pulled out that picture Annie had put under my pillow. "Check this out."

Angie looked at it and smiled, "Cuties. Look at that boy of yours. Old poker-face. He's your kid for sure, old 'stone-face Kelley'." She handed it back to me.

I stood, staring at it. I could never thank my lucky stars enough for having these two. Suddenly, I dropped my coffee cup. "Wait. It's the darn kids!"

I ran back to the fire, and confronted a sullen looking Al, "Let me see those tests you just ran."

He showed me the file on his handcompscreen, and I flipped through several 'pages' of results.

Angie followed behind me with my cup, "Kelley's flipped out, you guys. He's gone over the edge."

Out of the corner of my eye, I saw that slight grin on Tom's face.

He said, "Kelley's got something."

All the others started to gather around.

"It's the darn kids," I kept muttering. Satisfied, I took one more walk through the oak trees to get my story together. I already knew it, but now had to explain it. I walked back to see all six of my friends seated around the fire with the most hope of solving this riddle they'd had in years. "Al, get that large screenpad in the 'Beast' and link it to your handcomp. It'll be easier to see."

After setting it up, Al and I sat down on each side of the screen with the others facing us.

"Okay, I have to make several points here. They are in a chain. Let's start with point number one."

"I object," Al said, "let's call them by an appropriate title, assumptions."

"Okay. Assumption One. Patrick and Lilly left Leap Frog at the Old St. Louis site because they were in peril there. A man would risk a danger-filled scamp across the uninhabited prairie for no other reason. He certainly wouldn't be out hunting for illegal treasure. He went from a felt-minus situation to a felt-plus situation. I'm declaring this knowledge to be a priori."

"You can't just do that whenever you want to, Dan," Al said.

"I'm not going to argue with you, Al. I'm a dad and a dad would do anything to save his family. So, there.

"Assumption Two: Patrick knew the location of 'Destination A' before he left Old St. Louis."

"How do you know?" Angie asked.

"What's the shortest distance between two points?"

"A straight line," Wheeze said, smiling. "See, I know higher math."

Al laughed, "Actually, Wheeze, that's elementary geometry, but we're still proud of you." Wheeze beamed while Al went on, "But he didn't travel in a straight line, Sherlock." Al put up a map of Patrick's travels with a squiggly line leading to 'Destination A'. "See?"

181

"Okay, Al. Now put a straight line between the two points. Okay, now switch the map to the view that shows the topography." I pointed to the screen. "You see? While he meandered a bit, the average of these wanderings is a straight line. And look at why he did. Here's a lake he went around. Here's a river that he probably had to travel up to find a better crossing. Here's a swamp. He only meandered when he had to avoid barriers to the straight course."

"Okay. I'll buy that."

"Assumption Three: While my Dad knew where 'Destination A' was before leaving Old St. Louis, he didn't know where 'Destination B' was until he got to 'A'. He didn't know where 'C' was until he got to 'B', and so on. You see? It was a puzzle, a maze, a … oh, what was that game we played as kids?"

Angie added, "'Treasure Hunt'."

"Right. The players are led to some destination and it's there they get clues to the next stop. Pat was following a map, but a map that only showed itself while he traveled. The creator of this map either didn't want someone following my Dad or wanted to keep where he was going hidden."

"And," Tom added, "What led Patrick to his previous destinations is here on this hill."

I said, "Right. Assumption Four: Why did Pat and Lilly leave two little boys alone in the wilderness after the 'Beast' broke down? I kept thinking about Napoleon's horse. Pat knew they would all perish if he didn't reattach that solar panel. Plus, he needed my Mom to help him carry it or it might rip in the blizzard that was getting started. It was worth the risk. It was a risk he had to take."

"How did your parents die?" Wheeze asked. Then, realizing he may have said the wrong thing, he added, "I mean, if they died."

"Wheeze, it's okay. I assumed they perished long ago, for the same reason I used in Assumption One. They would not have left us there if something dire had not happened."

"You have one big, grand assumption left, my friend," Al said. "What was at those previous destinations, and what's here, that pointed their way?"

"Put that ground penetrating radar reading of the ground on the screen."

He did.

"We've been looking at this picture for eight years, guys, and none of us caught it. Anybody want to venture a guess?"

We all stared at it.

Ben concluded, "Those rocks? We've been through this, Dan. They look like a foundation of an old house or building. Some are scattered, probably due to groundwater or freezing and thawing."

"Anyone else?"

Clyde jumped to his feet, "These. See them? These four are lined up!"

"Bingo," I said. "These four form a straight line, a directional coordinate."

Now it was Al who got excited. "Let's go see."

Al was all smiles since I finally gave the scientist something he could understand.

We all ran out to the ground over those four stones. Al repeated his sounding, and calculated a line. We ran back over to the larger screen and he put it up. He drew a line from our spot here and extended it out toward the southwest.

"Okay, you are right. If he followed this heading, it would not lead straight back to Old St. Louis. However, it does intersect with 'Destination A', his first stop. So you're saying he would take this route home to Leap Frog? It makes sense since there is swampy land south of 'A' that he would be sure to avoid. That's why this line doesn't point directly back to Old St. Louis."

"That brings us back to the round trip theory," Angie added.

"But he made that note that he was heading back home after this stop," Al said.

"You're wrong, Al," I said, stunning my friends into silence. "Home is not that way. The line goes both ways, right? You drew the line right but you got the direction wrong. Home is in the opposite direction." I pointed to the northeast.

"How do you know that?"

"Bo Schlitz told us. Remember when he was up in that tree? He said the line goes both ways. He also said that home is where the heart is. Patrick's heart was not in Old St. Louis. He was in jeopardy there."

Tom said, "Dan, you do know Bo was having a psychotic break at the time?"

"Tom, do you remember at that Saturday night philosophy session we had last winter, when you talked about the Native American practice of a 'vision quest'? How did you describe the manner in which they prepared for that?"

"Yes. They went out into the wilderness, didn't eat or drink for several days, then visions came to them."

"And in more recent times some used the peyote cactus buds?"

"Yeah."

"That causes what kind of state?"

Dr. Pine thought for a minute, then smiled and said, "It causes delusions and hallucinations, similar to an acute psychotic state."

Clyde added, "Want to hear something spooky? Bo Schlitz loved the Eagles but adored Dan. He once said he and the rest of us saved his life. Bo was a withdrawn, schizoid kid in the seventh grade. We gave him friendship and security. One day he told me that he wanted so badly to 'help Dan with this puzzle,' but didn't have all the smarts that Al had. The doctor told us that Bo seemed to go off his meds on purpose; I wonder if he was trying to find an answer to this riddle in the only way he knew how."

I continued, "Right. He induced a psychotic state to escape the constraints of pure logic. He couldn't solve the whole puzzle, but at least wanted to give us some clues, if only on a symbolic level."

"And he probably doesn't even know he did. His memory of that terrifying time is gone, sealed over to prevent further damage to his psyche," Tom said.

We were all a little taken aback to see Dr. Al Myers wiping tears off his cheeks.

He said, "I feel awful right now. I get so caught up in intellectual pursuits that I sometimes forget how you guys, Bo included, helped make me what I am. None of what I have would have happened, if not for you guys. I have a friend like Bo Schlitz who would jump in front of a bus for me and here I sit doing math problems, totally ignoring him. I didn't even visit him in the stupid hospital!"

Ben said, "Cheer up, Al. Bo helped us; he aimed us in the right direction."

Al blew his nose, and then said to me, "Well, Dan, I hate to burst your bubble, but did you happen to realize that northeast of here there is absolutely nothing at all? Nobody's lived there for a thousand years or so. Did you also know that course would lead us all the way to the Atlantic Ocean? I hope you weren't planning to attend graduate school this fall."

"It's not that far. Al, put up that satfoto you took for me of our compound."

He put it up.

"Okay, draw a line from my back porch to that tree Bo had climbed up. Okay, now extend that line all the way down here. Great. Now, where that line there and the one you extended to the northeast from here intersect, that's where home is. That's where 'St. Patrick of the Prairie' was going."

"I'm afraid to ask, but how do you know this?"

"Annie told me."

"Annie? Your daughter, Annie? Two-year-old Annie?"

"Yeah. Bo told her."

"Well, that makes me a lot more confident in the source," Al said sarcastically. "That's in Indiana Territory, about as far as it is to down here from home. I'm going to have to be the devil's advocate here and ask: do you have a shred of physical evidence here? I mean you've come up with a series of assumptions, all based on the validity of the preceding ones, that to me is a house of cards. If you are wrong about any one of them, and there's certainly that possibility, then your whole theory comes crashing down."

"I can deliver that evidence."

"How?"

"Tomorrow morning, we dig down and take a look at one of those rocks. If there is nothing weird about it, if it is a fieldstone that's part of a foundation, I'll pack us up and we'll all head home. If not, then we all go to Indiana. Deal?"

Everyone nodded.

We were talking for so long it was beginning to get dark. Luckily we had some steaks to grill up. With an additional four or five day journey, most everything we needed to eat was going to have to be taken from the land.

It was premature to think about an extended trip until we dug up that rock. While the time passed since our conference, I gradually began to have doubts about what we would find. Perhaps those four stones were just part of a fieldstone foundation of a house or barn. Perhaps those particular stones somehow remained in a perfect line.

From my history studies, I had read about building construction in this area in the 18th and 19th centuries. After the homesteaders arrived, they began to convert the prairie into farmland. Each season, when they tilled the fields, they collected the rocks that had risen up from the earth's mantle or were deposited by glaciers. When they collected enough, they cut and stacked the rocks and utilized them for a foundation of a framed structure.

There were pros and cons about my theory. What fueled my doubts was that all the rocks down there were at the same depth. The GPR reading was grainy and showed little detail regarding shape. However, these particular four stones were so precisely lined up, they appeared to have been put there after the 'Youngest Dryas.'

After I cleaned my dishes, I walked out to meet Angie and Clyde, who were walking the perimeter again, this time they used the metal detector applications on their handcomps to check for clues. As complete darkness came over the site, they were about to give up.

"Find anything?" I asked.

"Naw, no gold around here." Clyde responded.

"Hey, I wanted to thank you two for going along with this. I know you probably want to go home."

Angie laughed, "Dan, nobody wants to go home. This is the most excitement we've had in years. Anyway, what I absolutely don't want to do is leave this riddle unsolved, and go back and talk about it for the next eight years. Let's get to the bottom of this."

Clyde said, "Hey, I'm a wildlife photographer. This is the way I live. I didn't even have to take time off work to do this; it is my work."

I slept very little that night, and every now and then I sat up and looked to the spot where those rocks were. Around three I got up and saw Clyde on watch. "Hey man, why don't you turn in early; I can't sleep anyway."

"I fully accept your offer," he smiled, "Angie's on duty at four."

But I never woke Angie. There was nothing to be gained by making her get up when I was wide awake anyway. I scanned the horizon while I walked; the almost full moon lit up the entire landscape. There was not an animal to be seen anywhere.

As the sun peeked over the eastern horizon and after a breakfast of venison steak with a side of venison steak, we all walked over to the spot. The four stones of interest were approximately three feet apart from one another. I determined it was only necessary to dig up one because I had a hunch they were all alike, and what was important was the shape.

Al asked, "Which one do you think we should dig up?"

"How about the one furthest to the southwest?" I said, "If my theory is correct, that would be the first one laid if indeed someone or something was trying to point the line to the northeast."

"Sounds logical," Al smiled at me. "We're going to make a scientist out of you yet, Kelley."

Clyde and Al took the first shift. We soon realized that those tiny foxhole shovels that came with the army gear were much less than ideal. Of course, they had to be compact for carry by infantry troops, but we now had the 'Beast'.

"What I wouldn't give for a real, long-handled shovel right now," Clyde complained.

We had to rotate shifts quite often, but we were progressing steadily. During a break, Al said to me, "You know what I think this stone we're digging up right now is?"

"What?"

"I think it's nothing but a cornerstone for a foundation. That's the first one put down and used to lay out the rest of the structure. In fact, these four may only be what was left of a wall that just happened to stay in line while the others scattered over the centuries."

"Well, we'll see pretty soon."

A four foot hole, with enough circumference to fit two people, proved longer to dig than anticipated. Angie relieved Al while Ben brought over water for the diggers. The sun rose and so did the heat.

Wheeze said, "You know, Angie, you're the only one the right size for that shovel."

She didn't respond, but chucked a shovel-full of dirt at him, hitting him dead in the chest, without even looking.

"Wheeze," Tom said, "never insult Angie while she has a weapon in her hand."

Soon, we heard the clinking sound of shovels striking stone. Clyde then squatted down in the hole to push away dirt with his hands. Then he said, "Okay, Angie, get down here and we'll lift it out."

She struggled and said, "It won't budge."

"Pry it up with your shovel."

"Too heavy for me," she said, "Bennie, I need you."

I was starting to shake like a leaf when Angie traded spots with her husband, and then Clyde and he bent down. With a few grunts and groans, the two got it up to their waists, then with a final effort, lifted the rock and set it on the dirt pile.

The seven of us stood in shocked silence. It was not a fieldstone, and certainly not part of any foundation. It was approximately a foot and a half across and several inches thick. It was hand cut into the shape of a perfect octagon!

Clyde was the first one to break the silence, "Just like those stones around Perimeter Road up on Thompson Defense Base that Dan was talking about. The story we dismissed in our meeting when Dan brought it up."

Wheeze asked, "When was it buried here?"

"About a hundred years ago," I said, "and I know by whom."

Ben added, "Okay, there was something very weird going on down here. In the 2950's some screwball stone mason traveled several hundred miles across this prairie and buried, four feet underground, twenty eight-sided rocks all pointing out a trail to nowhere."

"Or more scary yet," Clyde said, "to somewhere or something. These rocks are not visible from satellite or even an airplane. One would have to be sitting on top of them to figure out where each set pointed to."

Angie said, "Plus someone would have to know where 'Destination A' was to even have a chance of following the map."

"Do you guys remember my brother telling us he had a memory of Patrick O'Dea being excited over something he was reading?" I continued. "I think he was finding out about where he felt he needed to go and to find it by first finding 'Destination A.' This doesn't rule out someone being after him, but it does tell us that he had someplace to go. This wasn't a round-tripper, this was a one-way deal." I pointed to the northeast, "And that one way is thataway."

"Al," Ben said, "are you with us?"

Poor Dr. Myers was still staring at the rock with his mouth open.

He turned toward Ben and said, "I'm out of my realm here. From now on, whatever Dan says I believe; wherever he wants us to go, I'm going. He's doing a type of data analysis here I'm not familiar with. Let's go see what we can find over yonder."

The sun was beating down on us so intensely, we all decided to retrieve our wide-brim army boonie hats from our packs. We decided to rebury the stone. Clyde lifted it up to allow Al to chip a sample off the bottom for analysis back home. I'm not sure if we were being superstitious, but the rock had a purpose that we didn't want to mess with.

As Wheeze put it, "If the aliens find out we moved that rock, they're going to be awful ticked off at us."

We packed up and moved out immediately, not wanting to waste any time. Besides, the hill was not an ideal campsite. Al set the course into the 'Beast's GPS system and off we went with Tom and I on point.

Chapter 12

Even with the late start, we traveled almost fifteen miles that day. While the landscape looked much the same as it did just south of Old Chicago, the tree groves and the areas along the rivers became more fruitful. Roots, mushrooms, and even berries were plentiful. That night I made my most flavorful stew to date with wild grouse.

We maintained our brisk pace the next day, but the heat was bordering on unbearable. We found it easier to walk along the 'Beast' instead of riding inside, although there was no escape for the driver. Ben and Angie took shifts driving that day.

Later, Clyde spotted what looked like a lake about a half mile north of our course. Seven overheated and sweaty people wanted nothing more than to jump in that lake, so we headed in that direction. Angie and I were on point, and, unfortunately, with only her sidearm and my staff.

About twenty yards from the tree line, a large bison suddenly emerged that stood and stared at us. Our whole procession stopped in its tracks.

Angie reached for her holster, but I put a hand up to stop her from drawing the weapon.

"You're not going to stop it with that thing."

Luckily it was a cow and she appeared more curious than anything else. We slowly backed up toward the vehicle. However, a large bull came out next, and he was in a bad mood, and by big, I mean he was the size of a small bus and looked just as heavy.

Everyone remained quiet, and congregated around Clyde.

He whispered, "Okay, everyone slowly file inside."

One by one, we boarded the 'Beast'.

Inside, Clyde said, "We can keep the windows open but we have to remain quiet. That bull is more than capable of trashing this vehicle." He grabbed a laser weapon and stood up through one of the roof hatches.

Wheeze joked, "Clyde, bag it! We could eat for a month on one of those."

"No. I'm betting there's more by that lake over there. We'd start a stampede and they could easily roll this thing."

Our big, nasty friend snorted, pawed a front hoof on the ground, and looked like he was getting ready to charge. Then, he calmed down, and he and his 'girlfriend' started walking past the vehicle and slowly south. Then, more started to pop out of the trees and followed them. A few looked at us, but they all just glanced and moved on. We were soon in the middle of a giant herd that stretched more than a mile to the east and west of us.

A large cow stopped and looked right in the window at Wheeze seated in the driver's seat. "Holy crap," he said.

"Charm her, Wheeze," Angie said.

"Hi, sweetheart. Do you live around here?"

She kept staring at him.

"You wouldn't happen to know where a guy could get a good bison steak in this town, do you?" Then she snorted and walked off. "Women, huh?"

It took that herd the better part of three hours to pass us, while we sweated. After a while, we all had to relieve ourselves, but no one dared to get out. After the trailers were about a half mile away, Clyde called the 'all clear'.

After Wheeze pulled in next to the tree line, we all got out. Bison dung was everywhere and we soon discovered that the herd had trashed the lake. The water was muddy since the bison had probably taken a dip while passing through. What made matters worse, it was too late in the day to find another water source. We had to make a soup out of only two grouse breasts and the roots I had gathered.

The heat returned the next day. However, we did find a creek around ten in the morning and took a midday break to wash up and replenish the water in our tank.

Clyde and Ben walked upstream and came back with enough turtle meat to cram into the 'fridge'. Thank goodness, we had Clyde with us, because I wouldn't know the first thing about field dressing a turtle.

"This way we can stay on the road longer today," Clyde said.

It was ninety-six degrees at noon when we hit the trail again. After only about an hour, the slight breeze we had suddenly died out.

Clyde then noticed some dark clouds to the southwest. He announced, "There's a river up ahead, Wheeze, let's head over there. I think we have a storm brewing and we should hunker down."

The river ran east and west, but meandered south, so we headed for an oxbow. After we arrived, we hurriedly dug drainage channels around the 'Beast' and got ready for rain. The storm turned out to be a little more than we had anticipated.

Thick clouds soon got rid of that wicked sun, and we rejoiced in the reprieve. However, we soon noticed Clyde, who looked to the southwest through his field glasses for a particularly long time. High clouds began swirling about while the sky near the horizon turned jet black. Suddenly, this thin, black cloud shot down out of the sky, and hit the ground not more than a mile from us.

Clyde yelled, "Tornado! Get the packs and the laser weapons!"

Angie flew into the 'Beast' and started to throw packs out, while Wheeze and I secured all the windows.

"Shouldn't we get in?" Ben asked.

"No! Get to the riverbank!" Clyde yelled, while we all took off at a run.

"This isn't even true tornado season, Clyde." Al said.

"Do you want to explain that to the tornado?"

We all dove, stomach first, onto the bank. I landed next to Tom and we grabbed on to any vegetation we would get our hands on. The horrible sound was terrifying, like standing right behind a jet plane when it took off.

Suddenly, Angie flew over the bank, landing crosswise, right on top of Tom and me. Hail hit us and we heard projectiles hurling over our heads.

I felt Angie get lighter, and turned my head to the side and saw her slowly lifting off the ground.

"Tom! You have to save me - I'm floating away!"

Tom managed to get a finger through one of the belt loops in her pants and I grabbed an ankle, and pulled her back down. By this time it had turned pitch black and we could feel soil and twigs hitting us. Then, just as quickly as it arrived, everything turned totally quiet. We could hear debris hitting the ground after it escaped the grasp of the storm.

We all slowly stood up, and laughter broke out. We were a sight. Completely covered, head to foot, in a layer of black dirt, we looked like coal miners. Plus the hair on our heads was standing straight up and coated with dirt.

"Everyone okay?" Ben asked and we all nodded.

After getting to the top of the bank, we saw the 'Beast' still sitting there.

Wheeze commented, "The 'Beast'. There is no equal."

However, when we walked over to it, we saw that a tree branch had slammed against one of the solar panels and had smashed it to bits. Also, a stick with a diameter no bigger than one-half inch was driven right into the back right tire, flattening it.

As Wheeze and I climbed on top, he said, "Good. We have two spare tires and two spare solar arrays. We'll be okay." He picked up the branch that had smashed the cell and threw it off. Clearing some broken plastic away, he looked down into it. "Kelley, you're going to have to connect a new one. Darn, it's got water down in it; we'll have to dry it off."

He looked at Angie on the ground, "Hey Angie, did you bring a hair dryer?"

Our feisty friend looked up at us, "What do you think, Wheeze?" She pointed to her hair, "Do I look like I brought a stinkin' hair dryer? Maybe you guys would like to borrow my loofah while you're at it."

Wheeze then told me, "It's going to have to dry out. We'll fix it tomorrow. Let's get cleaned up."

That bath in the river was one of the best ones in my life. I must have sat in that water for an hour. The water was so warm from the recent heat wave that it was better than in a bathtub at home. I also got a change of clothes and scrubbed out the dirty ones.

We hung our clothes out on stakes and dined on some great turtle soup that Al and Clyde had made. The sun had come out just before it set. Off in the distance, we spotted a shining light on the ground to the southeast. Al said it must be the setting sunlight reflecting off a piece of foil that was blown in with the storm. Ben thought it was secret government agents signaling to one another. Wheeze suggested it was a little green alien with a flashlight.

Around the campfire that evening, we each told our own stories about the tornado.

Angie's was definably the funniest. "...and then I started to take off. I was yelling to Dr. Pine to save me, that I was flying off to Kansas. Al, where would I have ended up if that thing took me up in the air?"

Al said, "Oh, Lake Ontario or maybe even somewhere in Nova Scotia. But we would have come looking for you, Angie. It might have taken us a year or two, but we would have found you."

The next morning, Wheeze and I made short work of the tire change. However, I next had to tackle wiring that spare solar panel. I had notes on my handcomp from when 'Outlaw' and I wired them on, but I would have loved to have my quiet friend with me. The job took me over two hours. I barely had time for some breakfast, and then we were off again.

The tornado had gone southeast of us and we passed the one to two-hundred yard wide ditch it made on the prairie. The trees by where it crossed the river were either uprooted or completely missing. We could have easily all died in that storm and it was a sobering sight.

After only a few miles, the land turned to more dense woods and hilly terrain. We had to meander a bit around our course to keep on barren land. The vegetation changed also, with more bushes and taller grass.

Clyde joined me atop the 'Beast' and said, "Dan, you know those coordinates we're headed for are probably just a good estimate. A two-year-old pointing to the southeast is probably anything but precise."

"I know. I'm just hoping it's somewhere within sight of where we're heading. To make matters worse, I don't even know what we're looking for. What if it was a group of people? Why would they still be there after twenty years? I'm hoping it's some type of landmark."

"Or better yet some kind of rune stone. If August Viche was involved, it has to be something related to rock." Clyde put his hand on my shoulder, "But I thought of something funny last night. What if August was a practical joker? What if we find a ten foot monolith with these words carved into it: 'Ha, ha. I just sent you guys on an eight-year wild goose chase. Losers!'"

A little after noon, we stopped because Clyde had spotted a small gang of elk in the distance. Tom Pine and Clyde Hastings took a laser weapon and went out to chase them down. The rest of us sat on the ground near the 'Beast' and ate berries.

Angie said, "Al, how come scientists have such lousy senses of humor? Is it because you're thinking so hard about facts all the time that there's no room for fun stuff?"

"That's not true," he said. "We're very funny people."

"You never joke."

"What do you mean? We joke all the time."

"Tell us one," I said.

"Okay. I have one. Did you guys hear the one about the one-legged chicken? There's this guy, you see, who is down south driving on a country road. He is slowly driving along, looking at the scenery. Suddenly, he looks down and sees this one-legged chicken running alongside his car, hopping along. He's doing about thirty miles per hour. What the heck? How can this chicken run so fast? So the guy speeds up to forty, and the chicken stays right up with him. Then, he gets up to sixty, and the chicken is still running right next to the car. Fearing he might wreck his car, the guy finally slows down and the chicken goes running down the road and over the horizon. A little later, the car driver spots a farmer in his barnyard fixing his tractor. So he pulls in, gets out, and tells the guy, 'Hey, I just saw this amazing one-legged chicken!' The farmer says, 'Yeah, I know, I raise them.' So, the driver says, 'Wow. What do they eat?' The farmer says, 'Oh, just regular chicken food, ground corn and oats.' The driver asks, 'What do they taste like?' The farmer says, 'I don't know; I've never caught one!'"

We all sat quietly, staring at Al.

He said, "Get it? I don't know; I never caught one..."

"So what was the maximum velocity of the chicken?" Ben asked.

"That doesn't matter."

I asked, "Why would he raise them?"

"What was the name of the chicken?" Angie said.

Al stared at us for a moment, and then we all broke into laughter.

Angie patted Al on the shoulder, "Al, we used your joke to play one on you, and ours was funnier, by the way."

Clyde and Tom returned with as much elk meat that they could carry. My mouth began to water since elk is the prime rib of wild game. We would be having good 'eats' tonight.

We continued our journey. Ben and I sat atop the 'Beast', while Clyde and Angie took the point walk. Al rode inside, working on his joke delivery with Tom.

I loved these people. Attacking wolves, big river crossings, bison herds and tornados couldn't dampen their spirits or their desire to help me with this quest. Although I complained often about my family situation, I sometimes thought that the orphanage was a blessing in that I came across this group of people. My life would have very little quality without them.

The departing storm of yesterday ushered in a cold front, and the strong breeze and lower temperatures of this day were welcomed. However, the terrain was becoming hillier and more tree-covered. We were certainly entering deep woods. Al had a file of 'Old World' maps he used to keep us on a course over land that was used to grow crops. He attempted to avoid having us cross old metropolitan areas because of rubble piles and collapsing subterranean structures like residential basements or buried fuel tanks. While it was impossible to bypass all such hazards, hopefully our point people would see and report them to the pilot.

Clyde held up his hand and we came to a stop. He began to look up in the sky with his binoculars.

Ben and I saw it too; it was an airplane that was pretty high up.

Clyde walked back to the 'Beast' and said, "Plane."

"A commercial aircraft?" Ben asked.

"No, it's an Air Force jet fighter. Someone is keeping an eye on us."

"I knew it!" Ben said, "I think the government knows more than they were letting on."

I said, "It could be about either Patrick or the satellite hacking."

"I agree."

Since we already had dinner in the 'fridge', we did not stop until around five. Clyde found us a beautiful spot by a small, but deep lake, with plenty of trees. Angie and I set up camp while I kept thinking about some 'dynamite' elk steaks.

Wheeze and Al were looking at his 'Old World' map on his handcomp.

Wheeze said, "I don't know how much further we can go if this ground gets any worse. I'm already seeing exposed rock cliffs."

Clyde joined the conversation, "The usual broadleaf trees are thinning out and we're getting into more pines and firs. Plus, the game is becoming more abundant, so that's a good thing."

"Guys," I said, "my supper plans just have to include some wild mushrooms and roots. Can I get a bodyguard?"

Clyde and Angie agreed to come with me.

Clyde's stamina was something to behold. Not only was he on point most of the day, but he was even up for late-day hiking. He always said that this was his element.

We found a small spring just to our east, and followed it until we came to a low-lying, shaded meadow. Mushrooms and several varieties of berries were abundant. Clyde and I stood in the middle of the open area. I collected mushrooms, while Clyde stood guard.

Angie took to the bushes and started picking berries. "Which ones?"

"The pale red ones," I responded, "Not the bright red, those will kill you."

"Why don't you munch on a few, Angie?" Clyde teased.

"Why don't you eat a rock, Clyde? Hey, Kelley, these?"

I looked at her when she held them out. Something happened now, so fast, that nothing registered for a few seconds. An arm came out of those bushes and wrapped around Angie's neck! I straightened up while Clyde reached for his sidearm. We stood stunned, while one arm held our friend and another arm raised a laser weapon at us.

Angie gasped, "What the …"

With his face being somewhat blocked by the tall bushes, a man spoke, "Okay, nobody has to get hurt. I want you two to turn around and head back to your camp. Then, I'll let the girl go."

"Hey," Angie protested, "I'm a woman, you putz!"

Clyde whispered to me, "I can see there's no charge in that gun, plus the safety is on."

"Quiet!" he said, "You two separate."

We slowly walked a few feet from each other.

Angie struggled but he held on to her. Then suddenly, she shifted her weight to her left foot, swung around, and came up with a wicked right cross, landing right on the stranger's lower jaw. He flipped backwards and fell into the bushes.

Clyde was on him in an instant, grabbing the weapon.

We pulled our new 'friend' out of the bushes and onto the meadow grass. Although he had jet black hair and no beard whatsoever, he appeared older. What really struck me was that he had dark skin and was dressed in what looked like animal skin clothing.

He slowly came to, started moaning and holding his jaw.

I said, "Gosh, Angie, I thought you killed him."

"He scared the living crap out of me," she said, "especially when I saw that weapon."

The stranger muttered, "Did the girl hit me? For a minute I thought one of you shot me."

"I'm a woman!"

"You are a small woman, but you have a strong punch."

Clyde held his pistol on him, "Got any friends around here, buddy?"

"I live alone."

I said, "Pretty dangerous being out here alone with an uncharged laser rifle. I would hate it if you're lying to us. My friend here is awful good with that pistol, and you might make him mad."

"Would I have tried to grab the woman alone if I had more men around?"

He made a good point. "What's your name?"

"Mino."

Clyde said, "Is that your first or last name?"

He looked up at us, a bit confused and asked, "Why would anyone need more than one name?"

Clyde and I both calmed down. Mino appeared to be no threat at all. Come to think of it, during the momentary hostage ordeal he appeared more nervous that we did. However, I didn't want to give any details away just yet about why we were here. Our new friend might know something.

"As my friend said," Clyde went on, "why are you out here with no working gun?"

"I do most hunting with a bow and arrows. Didn't think I could pull this off with those, I needed both hands."

"Why do you want us to leave?"

"You can't go this way."

"Why?"

"I cannot say. I took an oath. These things are not for me to talk about."

I was going to try a new strategy with him. "Okay. Well, I don't want you to break your oath. If you are alone, do you want to join us for our evening meal?"

"No."

"We have fresh elk."

His eyes lit up and he asked, "You have elk? My camp is just over there. Can I get my things?"

Clyde seemed to know what I was up to, but also added, "Okay, but I'll go with you and hold on to those arrows for a while."

Angie and I quickly grabbed all the mushrooms we could and headed back to our camp.

We explained all that happened to our friends. Tom Pine was super excited, but Ben was less than thrilled at the course of action his wife had taken.

"Is the guy a Native American?" Tom asked.

"I think," I said. "He is older. I just can't believe he's out here by himself. He does have some secrets, that much is evident. He knows something he's not telling."

Ben said, "I think we should not give our hand away right now. Let's see if we can get some clues out of him. If he 'stonewalls' us, then we'll try something different."

Clyde and Mino came into camp, the latter carrying a leather sack, his bow, and a blanket. Clyde had the arrows and what looked like a hunting knife. Clyde pointed to Ben, "That's him."

Mino went to Ben and handed him a small pouch. He said, "Please accept this gift for the trouble I caused your woman. I had no intention of harming her. She really doesn't need the protection of such a big man." He rubbed his jaw. "Little woman has big fist."

Ben said, "I would certainly give this back to you for some answers about why you are here."

"I'm here because I live here. There is no other reason. Like I told your friends, I cannot talk further about this place or the happenings of this place. I have an oath."

"Okay. Please share a meal with us."

As our evening routine commenced, Mino sat on his blanket. We didn't know what to make of his accent. There was something very plain and unschooled about him. I had no idea what he thought of us. We traded insults and jokes with one another, so he must have thought we were crazy.

Wheeze teased Angie, "Little woman also has big mouth."

Angie sprung up into a fighting stance, "Hey, I'm 'Little Woman', 'Big Fist', and I punch, baby. Just ask Mino here."

For the first time we noticed a little smile on our new friend's face.

"Mino," she went on, "what do you think of Wheeze's tattoos?"

Wheeze unbuttoned his shirt and showed him. Mino didn't know what to make of those. He just starred with his mouth open.

Noticing an illustration of Wheeze's wife, he said, "Who's 'Mildred'?"

We figured he could read to some extent.

"That's my woman," Wheeze said, "She's Big Woman, Big Fist."

We all laughed.

As I was cooking, Mino was watching me. "You have skills."

"I try."

"Your fire is too hot."

He was right, so I let it cool down a bit.

While the rest of us stuffed ourselves with steak during dinner, Mino only ate half of one. He did seem to enjoy it, since he commented, "Elk is best."

Angie, known for her directness, asked, "So, Mino, do you have a woman?"

He looked down, "Long ago."

"Are you a real Indian?"

"Part."

"Have you lived here long?" Tom asked him. Mino appeared not to understand the question so Tom dropped it. "Has it been hot here this summer?"

"Yes, hot."

Tom tried to trick him, "How do you and the others keep warm in the winter?"

Mino caught on and just said, "I'll clean up." He picked up our mess kits and took them over to the lake to wash them.

Tom whispered, "Darn, he clammed up on me. This guy is a tough nut to crack. Any ideas?"

Wheeze responded, "I say he's an alien, and I think the mother ship is parked right over that ridge."

"I say we just go about our routine," Ben said, "and see if he slips up."

I said, "That oath seems important to him. I agree with Ben."

He returned with our clean mess kits and laid them out to dry. Then he walked around the 'Beast' and eyed it strangely.

We soon began to prepare our sleeping bags. While we placed ours under or near the awning, Mino preferred under the open sky.

"Aren't you worried about rain?" I asked.

"No rain tonight."

Al took the first watch while the rest of us joked around while we lay down.

Wheeze said to Clyde, "Have you heard the one about the one-legged chicken?"

"No," Clyde said.

"You're better off for it."

"Hey," Al complained, "that was a funny joke."

Angie spoke up, "Wheeze, say your prayers and go to sleep."

That only got Wheeze going more. He got up on his knees, put his hands together, and said, "Dear Lord, please bless this troop. Bless our great leader, Benjamin, for he not knoweth where he leads us. And bless his little runt of a wife ..."

"Hey!"

"... for she is now named 'Little Woman, Little Brain'."

She threw a rock at Wheeze, but missed. We even heard Mino chuckle a bit.

"Dear Lord, bless Dr. Myers. He is still playing with imaginary numbers, so please provide him with some real numbers someday. Bless Clyde, who spyeth thy tornado, and thy bison, and thy wolf who tried to eat me. Bless this group, we who honor thy name, who transverse the prairie in the spirit of St. Patrick O'Dea of the ..."

"Who?"

We all suddenly raised our heads and saw Mino, sitting up and staring at Wheeze. Our prayer leader was a little startled, "Who what?"

"Whose name did you say?"

We all suddenly sat up.

"Patrick O'Dea," Wheeze said.

"Do you know of him?"

"Heard of him."

"Have you heard of him?" Tom asked.

Mino looked serious, "Heard of him. Are you here about him?"

I decided I had enough of the games. I just said it, "I'm his son."

Mino asked, "You're Patrick O'Dea, the junior?"

"I'm his second son, Daniel. Yes, we're here about him and we're looking for where he was going."

"This changes things," Mino said. "I know where you need to go." He lay down and pulled the blanket over him. "We leave in the morning."

Chapter 13

No longer considered a threat, we returned Mino's arrows and knife the next morning. He remained silent when he took point, along with Ben, in front of the 'Beast'. But just in case, we had Clyde, armed with a laser weapon, sit on top and keep an eye on him. The only problem we had was his pace since Ben had to keep slowing him down. He was leading us off our original course, more due east than northeast. While we were not on a road or trail of any sort, Mino managed to keep us on ground the 'Beast' could handle.

Although our guide appeared to be a "prairie dog," to use the name Bob Wilson had in describing a person who could live entirely off the land, we doubted Mino was totally alone out here. Clyde thought him to be some sort of 'gatekeeper', someone we were led to by the stone map and needed to get to the real destination, where Patrick was headed. If we had not run into him, we would have followed that course to New England and wouldn't have found anything. However, the name Patrick O'Dea was not immediately on the 'tip of his tongue', but rather a remote memory or second thought. My Dad was more of a historical figure to the man. We did know, though, that Patrick was at one time headed to where Mino was taking us.

We got the impression there would be no lunch break, because Mino never stopped. Tom Pine then switched with Ben on point.

When Ben joined me atop the vehicle, I asked him, "Learn anything?"

"Little. He said we should be there in the late afternoon. He also told me that I talk too much."

"Yes, he seems like he's holding back on giving us any information about our destination."

Ben said, "Yeah, but I think it's because of that oath he said he took. I got the impression we are going to get more answers up ahead. I just wish I knew more about what was up ahead."

Early that afternoon, I lay down on one of the bunks in the back for a nap. After figuring out that sleep was not going to happen, I sat and looked out the window. The trees were getting denser, but we continued on a trail wide enough to accommodate our vehicle. Then, the path became narrower and narrower, until it was only slightly wider than the 'Beast'. I thought about those 'Old World' movies I had seen and couldn't help but feel this was a good place for an ambush.

After a while, I returned to a spot on top of the 'Beast'. I was getting more anxious with every foot we traveled. The trail widened a bit, but the surrounding forest grew denser. The wildlife was abundant; once, more than twenty deer hopped across the trail in front of us. Birds of all sorts sat on tree branches, sang, and watched the parade go by.

We came upon a bend in the trail that wound around to the right. Just before the trail bent back again to the left, at the extreme angle of the bend, Mino held up his hand and Wheeze stopped the vehicle.

Tom walked back from point to announce, "He wants us all out of the vehicle."

We all lined up in front of the 'Beast,' while Mino stood about ten yards in front of us, and faced down the trail. My heart was racing.

Then from around the bend, a lone woman appeared and stopped in front of our guide. She was tall, with long black hair, and with dark skin like Mino. However, her facial features appeared more Polynesian, and she was drop-dead gorgeous. We stood, transfixed.

Wheeze gasped, "Oh, my gosh, she's enough to make ya wanta join the tribe."

"Okay, you 'wolves'," Angie said, "need I say, that most of you have wives and girlfriends?"

Al said, "I don't." He stood looking at her with total infatuation.

She spoke, "Who goes?"

"I, Mino."

"Who do you bring?"

"Friends."

"What do you know of their character?"

"They gave me food, shared a fire," Mino answered, then turned around, pointed at me, and waved me up to join him.

As I walked toward him, I couldn't believe how corny this whole greeting thing was, like a script from a bad, old Western movie, but I felt I was getting close to something, so I didn't let on.

Mino said, "This is O'Dea."

The woman stared at me, expressionless. We must have stood there, quietly, for a full minute.

Then she started to turn, and said, "Follow me, bring your vehicle" and began walking down the trail.

My companions returned to the 'Beast' and started after us, while I walked in front of it. Mino stood to the side to let us pass. Realizing I had forgotten my manners, I turned to thank our strange friend only to see that he was already gone.

We came to where the trail bent around again to the right. There was another bend up ahead, about a hundred yards or so. Through the trees I saw something bright just beyond them. Although the sun was behind us, I couldn't help but think it was some sort of light.

As I turned into the final bend in the trail, we came before a wide river. It wasn't deep by any means, and I saw our new guide was already halfway across. I climbed onto the ladder next to the driver's window.

Two large rock cliffs faced us, almost pale white in color, with a canyon in between. Small trees and vegetation covered the top of the rocks. We exited the river on the other side and proceeded through the valley. The canyon walls gradually turned to wooded hills about fifty feet tall with occasional trails that led up into the trees.

I hung onto the ladder while we traveled up the canyon toward the east, and noticed small huts at the bottom of the hills on each side. The dwellings had roofs of foliage stitched together with vines. People dressed in buckskin sat in front of them, and mostly stared at us. Some of them had dark skin and some looked like us. We saw one fair-skinned male with flaming red hair. The place reminded me of Dr. Principi's Paleo-Indian exhibit in the history department lobby.

I heard Al say from inside, "Did we just pass through a wormhole somewhere? These people look like Holy Cross on steroids."

"I had imagined if we actually found people out here, they would be advanced," I added. "This appears to be several steps backward."

Our guide stopped in front of one of the huts, we also stopped and got out. Out walked an older lady who wore a long dress and used a cane. She had white skin. She stopped, then looked at me, then fainted. After she went right down to the ground, our guide and a man exited from the hut and ran to her. I just stood and watched, not knowing the protocol here, while they carried her into the dwelling.

"Way to go, Kelley," Angie said, "First I knockout Mino, and now you drop the old lady."

We waited a few minutes, and then our guide exited the hut and spoke to me, "'Mother' is ill. She'll talk to you in the morning. You can put your vehicle next to the lean-to over there."

I was getting quite frustrated, "I need some information here."

"You'll get it in the morning." She walked across the canyon to a hut on the other side.

Wheeze pulled the 'Beast' down to the shelter, and the rest of us walked along. I was growing weary of these constant delays and needed some answers pretty soon.

On the south side of the valley, Wheeze parked the vehicle facing west. We pulled out our awning and set up camp.

Clyde found a nice stack of firewood and got a fire going. I was just about to get the cooking equipment, when two men approached with large ceramic dishes loaded with food. Everyone welcomed a meal already cooked.

As we ate, I said, "She called the older woman 'Mother'. They don't look related."

"I got the impression that it was a title," Tom said. "This is a strange place."

Ben added, "Well, we're setting a watch tonight. Everyone is so closed-mouth around here; it gives me the creeps."

"I don't think they're going to give us a gourmet fish dinner and then kill us in our sleep, Ben," Clyde said. "Gosh, this fish is broiled. They must have stone ovens."

As darkness fell, we also noticed no indication they had electricity out here.

"Well," I added, "I'm not leaving here until I get some extensive information."

We noticed our female guide with another woman outside a hut across the way, while she ate dinner. Al was staring at her.

"Gee, Al," Angie said, "Go talk to her."

"I think I will." He got up and walked over.

Containers of fresh water were also delivered. We washed our mess kits and ourselves before unrolling our sleeping bags. Ben assigned me the four o'clock watch because he knew I'd be up.

Al returned after setting up a meeting for tomorrow afternoon with the guide. He also mentioned some of the elders would be meeting with us in the morning. I hoped they would be much more talkative.

I must have underestimated the energy I had expended the previous day since Angie had a hard time waking me up at four. I sipped tea someone had provided and walked around our small camp. While we had kept an eye on our hosts all night, they were doing the same to us. I spotted their watch up in the trees on the facing hillside.

At 5:30 a.m., Al Myers got up and poured himself a cup of tea. He motioned me to follow him out into the center of the valley, out of earshot of the others.

Once reaching a safe distance, he said, "Dan, don't tell Angie or the guys about this, okay? I'll never hear the end of it. I need your help. I don't know what to say to this woman."

"The one who led us in here? What do you mean?"

"Well, what do I talk about?"

"Al, you've talked to women before."

"In the math lab! We swap transcendental equations instead of phone numbers. This one is special. She's a wilderness girl."

"Okay, don't worry about what she is - that's inconsequential. You're a man and she's a woman. Tell her about yourself and then ask her about herself. Find out what she's interested in. I don't know, ask her what her favorite bird is, but most of all relax."

At approximately six o'clock, more trays of food arrived while I aroused my companions. This time they brought real pancakes, with real syrup and real pork sausage. We devoured our meal since we hadn't seen a pancake in many days. Most of our breakfasts on the trail consisted of whatever we had the night before.

After cleaning up, I sat on a rock and waited for the older lady to come out. Finally, she appeared from out of the doorway and waved me over.

I approached her, and tried to keep an emotional lid on my expectations. I may have been in for more of "heard of him" or "didn't really know her" or more of the same thing I had been hearing about my parents all these years.

217

She reached her hand out to me and said, "Hi, you must be Daniel. You can call me 'Mom'." A shudder went through me.

I shook her frail hand and, noticing my reluctance, she added, "Don't get the wrong impression; I'm not related to you. I'm the matriarch of the people here. My full title is 'Mother', but there is no need for formalities. Will you walk with me?"

I held out my arm for her to take and she did, smiling at my offer. We walked to the east of her hut, and then headed into a steep valley in the hill wall. We soon came in sight of another massive river, this one wide and deep. The lady didn't appear that elderly, more like sick. She wore a massive wide-brim hat and a long dress.

"This is the Wabash River," she said, "It's so pretty here. I figured we would start our talk today with a history lesson."

"You know, 'Mother', I mean 'Mom'. With all due respect, I've gathered more history about my parents than you probably know. I've taken months, years, learning about this clue and that. I've traveled too far, too long. I need to know what you know about them, and I need to hear it pretty soon."

She didn't pull any punches. "Very well. Daniel, your parents are deceased."

I stopped in my tracks, knees wobbling slightly and my eyes filling up with tears. It was the first time anyone had ever said that. "Okay. I mean, I mean I figured that. When?"

"September 3, 3055. More precisely, probably five or ten minutes after they left you to go get the solar panel."

"How did they die?"

"They were assassinated. They were shot with a conventional rifle."

"Who did it?"

218

"A man by the name of Leo Gustav, and I have no idea why."

I stood there, and tried to make sense of all of this. "I ... I don't agree. Leo Gustav headed north of Old St. Louis that year to retrieve some chainsaws. He went missing after that trip."

"Leo Gustav came after your father."

"Okay, how do you know all this?"

"Because I was with the party that found your parents. Your dad had a radio and put out a call that he was broken down. We were thirty or so miles east of him, out there to meet him after he got the coordinates on that hill with the stones. We had a radio then, heard it, and came to find him.

"By the time we got there, you kids were gone. We found the bodies and also found the tracks the murderer made when driving off. Two of our men tracked him for two days. They found the dune buggy he was driving. He had hit a tree stump and the vehicle flipped over on itself and hung down the side of a riverbank. They found Gustav's body; he had gone through the windshield. The men also found the weapon he used. They buried the body and brought the rifle back with them."

"So the buggy is still out there?"

"Well, it's in the river now. About a year later some of our people were out there and noticed the dune buggy had dropped into the river. The body's still out there if you want to go dig it up."

"Where did you find my parents?"

"About a mile southeast of their vehicle. At first, we thought the killer grabbed you two boys and killed you both. We didn't know that you were in Centura until years later."

"Who made that satcall to Thompson?"

"That information is going to have to wait for the history lesson. Come with me."

We walked up a slight rise to a grassy, level area overlooking the river. We approached a white stone, about four feet tall and two wide. When we came around to the face of the stone, I read the inscription:

Here lies Patrick and Lilly O'Dea

Who returned to the earth, 3 September 3055

I immediately fell to my knees, then fell forward, prostrate on the ground. I cried. The tears started pouring out so fast I didn't have time to control them nor any will to. 'Mom' couldn't get down to console me, but she came nearer and spoke in a soft, kind voice. "I know you probably often considered this, but today it's become real."

So I lay there, 'watering the grass'. I found myself crying aloud. After remaining there for twenty or thirty minutes, the tears finally abated. I propped myself up on my forearms and looked over to see the woman sitting quietly on a rock.

"We brought the bodies back here. This is where they were coming and we figured this is where they wanted to be."

Slowly getting to my feet, I walked over and joined her on the rock. "That was hard to hear. I'm sorry."

"For what? For being human?"

As I blew my nose in my handkerchief and composed, she went on, "I need to give you that history lesson now."

"'Mom', I have a friend who is a philosopher in our group, and he would sure want to hear this too."

"Two of our elders are meeting with your friends this morning, and are explaining all this."

220

We gazed at the river a moment before she continued, "First I will tell you what we are not. No, we're not a religious cult. No, we are not a lost tribe of Israel. No, we do not advocate the overthrow of the U.S. government by force. We are noncompetitive; we're dropouts. We have been out here for a hundred and fifty years. Not right here, mind you, but around here. Long ago a group of men got together who were unhappy with the civilization we rebuilt after 'The Chaos'. They saw the disasters of the mini-ice age and the 'Blue Solution' as a second 'Noah's flood,' if you will. They realized we were making the same mistakes we did before. These men traced it all the way back to when we transitioned from hunting and gathering to agriculture. Our forefathers came up with a radical plan."

"Don't you mean 'foremothers'?"

"No, they were men."

"I thought you were matriarchal. Why would men give up their dominant role in society?"

"Because what we were doing was a mistake. We made that error before. Ever wonder if Genghis Khan's wife would have been in charge, what things would be like? What if Mrs. Bonaparte ran things? She would have said, 'Russia? I'm not going to Russia. It's too cold there and anyway I just washed my hair.'" She looked at my astonished expression and said, "That's a joke. Don't you still have those in civilization?"

I laughed. I began to realize my lecturer was quite a character.

She went on, "I was using an exaggerated example to make a point. What's the term the philosophers use?"

"I think it's a reductio ad absurdum."

"Yeah, that. We got rid of Latin, too. I never did care for it. Anyway, we became matriarchal for a reason. Our forefathers subtracted all the things from society that weren't working, and what was left over is what you see here.

"Take capitalism for example. It implodes. Henry Ford figured that out. It's called engineered obsolescence. Long ago, they made a widget that cost one hundred dollars and lasted for ten years. Later, they made them for seventy-five dollars and they lasted five years. Humans beat themselves on the chest and said, 'Look at us; we're saving twenty-five bucks on widgets!' They never sat down and did the simple math."

"So, you're saying socialism or anarchy is better?"

"No. I'm saying - Get rid of the 'ism's!' What's wrong with bartering? We have everything we need.

"People celebrate the best, don't they? We have the Nobel Prize, Miss America, and the championship game. Civilization worships a status ninety-nine percent of the population will never experience. Not here. No, we have no extensive libraries, or art museums. We don't celebrate the best. The ones who survive out here, Daniel, are the most average. We don't produce great things, just great people."

"How do you get people?"

"Many are just born here. Others are recruited. We have three criteria for joining us: A person must be unhappy with civilized life, know how to live in the wild, and leaves no sign behind of their destination."

"Aren't you worried that you'll be discovered?"

"People are hard to see if nobody is looking for them. The folks in civilization are busy with their computers and their satellites and all the stuff that got the human race in such a mess to begin with."

I asked, "Are you pure hunter-gatherers?"

"Not pure. You might say we have such tendencies, but we also grow gardens and raise some animals. Sort on the cusp of nomads and villagers."

"So, a new recruit has to find his way here. He would need a map. That must be where August Viche came in!"

"You figured that out, huh? You have a good mind, Daniel."

"Yeah, thanks. Do you want to hear how I figured that out? I saw his name on a plaque on the side of a building. With all my 'analytical ability', I stumbled upon it by accident. I only saw it because I was standing under the portico waiting for a ride. What we couldn't figure out about his map, however, is how does someone figure out the distance between signposts?"

"They are equal distances." she said, "The distance between the start near Old St. Louis and the first set of stones is equal to the distance between all the others. So the few people who gained knowledge of where the start was had to keep track of the distance. The information your father had was the start point, the location of the first stones, and the distance between them. I'm not going to tell you where that start point is because you obviously don't need it now."

"So how do you find people? How did you know about my Dad?"

"There used to be more of us out here than you see today. Once we were nearly two thousand. We had people out in the real world also. We got information to him. Patrick was a jack-of-all-trades and he could live off the land. Your mom was from here, though, did you know that?"

"No."

"She was born out here with us. When she was just a baby, the elders noticed something wrong with her eyesight. They wanted to give her a chance for a life with sight, so two men took her overland to a hospital in Tennessee. She had her eyes fixed and was put up for adoption. After marrying your dad, she ended up on her way back here with no memory of the place."

"I interviewed an elderly man that had met her and he said he never heard her speak. Could my Mom speak?"

"I'm pretty sure she could. Maybe she just didn't have anything to say to the man."

"It's funny. Mino even commented that we talk a lot."

"Mino conducts himself in the old ways. He is one of our people who live out in the periphery. We used to have more. He's lived alone in the woods since he was twelve. It's a sad story actually. He fell in love with a young girl once; he was sixteen and she fifteen. They wanted to marry, but her parents didn't approve of such a young marriage. So, they ran off together to live in the wild. In less than a year, she was struck by lightning and died. He's lived alone since, and rarely comes in here. He wants to be close to her spirit for his love for her is as strong as ever. Such behavior would be considered foolish by civilized people, but it's a definition of love they have forgotten about.

"Mino probably complained to you that white people talk too much in general. He's distrustful and thinks small talk is a waste of time. I found a way to get along with him. I frame a paragraph in mind of what I want to say to him, and then subtract everything that's meaningless."

I said, "Forgive me for coming up with things sporadically, but I want to ask you some things and I'm bringing them up when they come to mind. Was Governor Viche related to August?"

"Yes, he was a descendent. Gov grew up here, by the way. He was one of those people in the real world I was telling you about earlier. He wanted to go try it. The people tried to tell him he wouldn't like it out there. He was grossly disfigured and they thought he would suffer for that since so much emphasis is put on appearance. I received word that you were instrumental in revealing his killers."

"It was a hunch, too."

"Mino knew him and was fond of him. You got elevated to cult status, Daniel, when he heard you resolved that issue."

"Do you have a family, 'Mom'?"

"No, I don't."

"Is there some connection there with you being the matriarch, and all?"

"Oh, no. I just never married. To tell you the truth, I never met a man I could stand for more than a week or so. I have a boyfriend now, but I just keep him around to kill snakes and spiders."

We laughed and I continued, "I almost hate to bring this up, but there are several departments of the military that are interested in how that satellite SOS call got through."

"As I said, we had more people here long ago. We had one who was a 'mad scientist,' by mad, I mean totally crazy. When he found us, he professed his desire to give up his old ways and convert to our way of life. But as he became ill, he started tinkering around with some electronics he found in an underground storage facility somewhere. He messed around with all sorts of electronic stuff. This was back at our winter home in the caves. He developed a satellite receiver that could pick up television and the quantanet. I also heard he was working on a transmitter. The elders at the time told him not to mess with that. Your dad was a highly sought-after recruit, with his young wife being from here, and children and all, as our numbers were starting to diminish. We had people pretty much all over the area then with those radios, and when Patrick made that call, it was relayed back to him. I guess he used that as a test call on his transmitter. I don't know how he did it. One of the elders is trying to explain it now to your scientist."

"What ever happened to him?"

"He committed suicide. I told you he was ill. He had said he always wanted to drown himself in Lake Erie. I never cared much for his choice of Great Lakes. I would have chosen Huron or Superior, one with a little more romance attached to it. Anyway, a year later that's where some of our people found him, washed up on the shore of Lake Erie. They took apart the transmitter and buried the parts because we figured the government would come looking for it. We discarded the radios after that as well, in fear of someone tracking a signal."

A man came carrying a platter of roots and nuts, and left it for us to snack on. She ate some of it but it didn't look like it agreed with her.

She asked, "Have you noticed anything peculiar about the people here?"

"Yes, I noticed there are few young people around, no kids at all."

"Our little society is dwindling down, Daniel. There are probably no more than forty of us left out here. It is difficult to recruit because so many of our people out in the real world have died or are becoming elderly. The young leave. I won't be around much longer."

"What's wrong?"

"I'm ill. Our doctor died over a year ago, now. Before that he said I have a terminal disease and probably wouldn't last long. After I'm gone, this band here will probably scatter."

"Are you in pain?"

"It's almost constant now. I can't sleep for more than an hour at a time, so it takes a toll on me."

"Mom, why don't you come back with us? I don't know what's wrong with you, but even in the worst case, you shouldn't have to spend your last days in pain. They have stuff for that."

"Oh, I've never lived anywhere else, so I guess I'll stay. I am going to have to go back to my hut now. Will you walk with me?"

We stood and she took my arm again. I felt terrible.

"If I'm too ill in the morning, there will be an elder or someone around to answer any more questions you may have. Please stay a day or more, talk with the people, rest up for your trip home. Please be discrete with what you learn here. The only reason we accepted your visit was out of respect for your dad, and that I wanted you to know about him. Mino knows the story well."

I led her to her hut entrance, where two older men took over at the door. I turned around and slowly walked back toward our camp.

My six friends were all standing there, in a line, with arms down at their sides as if at attention. I walked before them and stood there. Some looked at me, some down at the ground. I had no words for them, but none were expected. One by one, they walked up to me.

Wheeze hugged me and said, "Sorry to hear about your folks, man."

After Wheeze got back into line, Clyde came forward, placing his hands on my arms, "I'm proud to call their son my friend."

Then Al said, "There are no math equations for this, Dan. I wish I could calculate one to make you feel better."

"I've been chasing down Patrick and Lilly with you for so long," Ben said, "that it feels like I just found out my parents had died. You will always be my brother." He hugged me.

Tom then came forward and hugged me also. "We've been down this road a long time, you and I. From the moment I met you, I knew you were destined to go to the ends of the earth. I was happy you let me come along; I was never in better company."

Angie came up and hugged me tightly. She was bawling and that got me started all over again. "They are here, Danny. This is where they wanted to be, and they are resting here now."

We stood facing each other once again. I could only say, "I've had a long day. I'm tired." I lied down on my sleeping bag and fell asleep.

After waking, I spent the rest of the day sitting by our fire and trying to make sense of all this. My friends sort of let me be. Then, I turned in early.

I finally regained consciousness at seven the next morning, and then only by the noise Angie was making washing out mess kits in a ceramic water pot.

"Oh, glad you could join us, you lazy moron." Angie's empathy only goes so far.

However, I was glad. I didn't want to turn this whole visit into a wake. These people were exciting and I was looking forward to learning how they lived.

"Did I miss my watch?" I asked her.

"No, Ben suspended the watches last night. One of their guys was on duty so he didn't see the need. I saved you some breakfast. Waffles, can you believe it?"

Clyde stopped by with one of their men on their way out on a hunt. He told me it was decided to spend a couple of days here before heading back. This suited me just fine.

After I finished eating, I sat and sipped tea. Then I saw Al Myers walking toward us with the woman who led us in here. They were laughing.

Al introduced her, "Dan, meet Tina." I reached up to shake her hand. He went on, "Tina has a Ph.D. in anthropology from the University of Miami."

She smiled at me, "So, you're the one?"

"One what?"

"You're the one who told Al here to ask me what my favorite bird was? Really? You couldn't come up with a better pickup line than that?" They laughed while I sat there blushing. She looked at Al and said, "History majors. They're all alike. They aren't worth a darn in the present."

After they sat down to join us, I asked her, "Tina, how did you come to join these people?"

"Well, I did a lot of field work in some very remote places with some small bands of people who lived on the edges of civilization. This was mainly in Kentucky Territory. I learned a lot about surviving out in the wild. Soon, I began to like it in the field more than at the university. I became dissatisfied with modern life and heard a legend about a group of people living in the wild up north. So, here I am. I may go back someday, who knows?"

The events of the day proved very informative for all. Clyde and Wheeze spent the day hunting, Angie with one of their horticulturists, and Ben and Tom with one of the elders. Al, of course, spent his day with Tina. I hung out with two of the most amazing cooks I had ever met. They showed me actual cooking herbs that could be found in the forest and roots I had never seen before. These roots had always been in abundance everywhere, I just had not known where to look.

In the afternoon I took a turn with an elaborate stone cooking stove. It was probably eight feet tall and six feet in circumference. They had made it all with just hammers and chisels. The biggest challenge was keeping the interior at just the right temperature. While my first two loaves were a disaster, later in the day I was putting out bread like a seasoned baker. We ate a good deal of it that night at dinner.

The next day was spent preparing for our trip home. I began to see a bit of homesickness in my friends' faces. I was missing Marie and the kids, too. Our friends gave us pemmican and some of their homegrown tea to take back with us. Our coffee was gone. Wheeze greased up the 'Beast' and checked the fluid levels, while I tested all the electrical connections.

Later that evening, I made one last visit to 'Mom's hut. I found her lying on a bed with her head raised. She was in pain, I could tell, but managed a smile. "Are you leaving tomorrow?"

"Yes. We'll be taking off rather early, so I wanted to stop by this evening. You know, that offer to come with us still goes."

"I know. Thank you. You take care of yourself, Daniel, and take care of that great family of yours."

"I will. Thank you for helping me with this." I hugged her.

She said, "May the Creator go with you."

"Is the Creator and God the same being?"

She just smiled, "What's in a name, aren't we talking about the same thing?"

Chapter 14

I was out at my parents' gravesite at 4:45 the next morning. I squatted down and touched the headstone with my hand.

I was startled to hear, "Saying goodbye?" It was Angie.

"I don't know if it's goodbye or hello. You know, I often thought I'd find them alive down here, living in the forest like Tarzan and Jane, but I had two different scenarios."

"What were they?" she asked.

"Well, in the first one, I'd smack my Dad right in the mouth, curse at my Mom, and scold them both for making me grow up in that orphanage, but in the second one, I'd hug my Dad, kiss my Mom, and tell them all about my interesting life. I would even show them pictures of their grandkids."

"Somehow, Dan, knowing you, I think you would have done the second thing." She stood next to me and put her hand on my shoulder. "They couldn't help what happened. At least they didn't do what my husband's parents did and leave you on a doorstep. Now you're in charge. You have to go back and take care of those two little ones that you have. You have to give them birthdays and Christmases and all the other special days you didn't have, and on Father's Day, let Annie bring you a dish of ice cream. Let her honor the man who, with his last dying breath, won't ever let anything bad happen to her."

"That may be the most profound thing you ever said to me."

"I have my moments. Do you know why I give you guys such a hard time? Ever wonder about that? It's because you sit around that campfire and eat that fatty meat and talk about the old days. When motivated, the Eagles are some of the smartest men I know, but you need a fire lit under you to get you moving. When I heap my 'good-natured' insults on you, you guys fire them back, but you need a catalyst."

I stood up, "Really? Here, I thought you were just a pain in the neck."

"Oh yeah?" She grimaced, cocked her head to the side, and put her hands on her hips. Then she burst out laughing.

We started walking back to the camp, "You can be a nice person, Angie, but then again, you're not really a whole person. You're not even half of one."

"Oh yeah?"

"I think about the only thing you're good for is making watches for real little people."

"Oh, a watchmaker? You know what, Kelley? You're such an idiot; you're an insult to all the other idiots."

"Oh yeah?"

"Yeah. Other idiots have told me this."

"You know what, Angie? ..." We traded insults all the way back to camp.

We had everything and everyone loaded on the 'Beast' and ready to go. Ben had come up with a great idea to cut down on our travel time home. We would go almost due north to Lake Michigan, and then take the beach north to Centura. This saved us the three days it would take to go completely around Old Chicago to the west.

Dr. Al scored a kiss from Tina just before he hopped on the already moving 'Beast'.

Ben then yelled to her, "How will we find Mino?"

"Just go out the same way you came in; he'll find you."

Sure enough, out on the narrow trail we took to get here, there stood Mino with his bow and arrows. He joined Clyde on point. After only about a mile, we turned north.

Most of us guys either rode outside or walked behind while Angie attended inside. Ben, Al, and I sat on the roof of the vehicle.

"Are you two ever going to get together again, Al?" I asked.

"Don't know. Maybe. She was pretty intent on staying there for now."

"Did you get the scoop on how that 'mad scientist' hacked that satellite?"

"I did. It was such a simple thing I'm not sure why hackers never tried it before or haven't since. He 'double-barreled' it."

"Can you explain that in English?"

"Yes. This all happens at the speed of light, but for our discussion here we'll look at it in slow motion. Now, when an authorized sending station sends a message to a satellite, it sends it in a single string of ones and zeros. If it is not an authorized signal, the blocking mechanism on the satellite will reject it. What this guy did was set up two transmitters, let's say about a mile apart, and sent the identical message up simultaneously. Let's call them 'transmitter A' and 'B'. When the blocker looked at the signal coming from 'transmitter A', it saw it was phony, and rejected it. Then it switched to look at 'B,' but while it was looking at 'B', part of 'A' was not blocked. Then, it switched back to 'A' and part of message 'B' got in, and so on. So, what the satellite did accept was half of 'A' and half of 'B'. However, they were opposite halves. So, what got transmitted to Thompson were two halves, but to the receiver it looked like one single message. Since it did get transmitted, it looked official. It drove the satellite 'crazy' because no one ever sent messages that way before."

Ben said, "Genius."

"Now, I'm sure he did a bunch of other stuff with the code. I don't know and I don't want to know. Doing this is against the law. You guys know, I hope, that I'm duty-bound to report this to Mr. Durham."

"Yeah," I said, "but let me be with you when you explain it. Ben, I've been meaning to ask you, what was in that pouch that Mino gave you?"

"Tobacco. Can you believe it? What am I going to do with it?"

I answered, "I think it was just a meaningful gesture."

"We saw the meaningful gesture Tina gave you, Al," Ben added, then asked me, "Well Dan, it turned out your dad was not a gold smuggler, a spy, or an alien. Are you disappointed?"

"Not at all. He was just an average guy doing what he thought best to save his family. I couldn't be prouder."

The journey went well. The next day I took point with Mino, and, following 'Mom's advice, didn't talk too much. I noticed him smiling more that day and found that we communicated just fine without a lot of small talk. He pointed out things to me when he wanted me to note something.

He asked, "Are you going to change your 'second name' to 'O'Dea' now?"

"Probably not. My wife and kids are named 'Kelley'. What's in a name anyway? It's just a label; I already know who I am."

Mino smiled.

At the end of two very long days on the trail, Mino led us to the top of a hill that overlooked Lake Michigan. Although we urged him to spend the night in camp with us, he insisted on being on his way.

He gave me a double handshake, "Dan is a friend."

"Mino is a friend," I said.

Then, at a steady run, he disappeared into the forest.

We got down to the lakeshore by six the next morning, only to see our great plan fall apart. We stood and looked at a disaster. While the military and Centura city workers kept our beaches spotless, the shoreline down here was strewn with tree limbs and trash and everything else that had been blown down by north winter winds. It was completely impassable.

"Well, Einstein," Angie asked, "what do we do now?"

"We can't get through that," Wheeze said, "If we took a slightly more inland route we'll run into the rubble piles. Guess we'll have to go around." Then he thought for a moment. "Wait, there may be a way."

"How?" Ben asked.

"Anchors aweigh, my boys."

Angie had a fit, "No way! Go out on the lake? That's a big lake."

We looked at the expanse of water.

"Yikes," I said, "It sure looks a lot bigger today."

Ben looked at Al, "What's your estimate?"

He fiddled with his handcomp. "Twelve, thirteen hours."

"It's a calm, sunny day, guys," Wheeze added. "We could be in a hot shower and clean sheets by 7:00 p.m."

"We have extra weight, Ben," Clyde said.

"Let's give it a shot. We'll take a short test run and if it doesn't go well we'll come back and go around."

"You're nuts, Ben," Angie said, "If I drown out there, I'm never forgiving you!"

"Maybe I should apologize in advance."

So, we 'fearless sailors' took to the 'sea'. Ben decided to keep the same setup as the river crossing, with me riding just above the cockpit, he on the stern, and the rest inside. I don't mind admitting that I was quite anxious.

Wheeze did have a depth finder that, when angled forward, warned him of approaching submerged obstacles. He did follow the coast, but kept about a quarter to half a mile out to avoid old sunken wrecks that might be near the shore. When he got up to the speed he felt he could handle, it was actually a pretty smooth ride. It did take me about an hour to get used to it.

We continued northward, and the eerie landscape of Old Chicago came into view. The very tall rubble mounds made the landscape appear like a mountain range. I couldn't help but think of what it must have looked and sounded like when those skyscrapers collapsed.

Around noon, Angie poked her head out of one of the hatch holes and gave Ben and me some bison jerky to munch on and water to drink. She didn't stay and visit. The water was calm but the view from our tiny boat on such an immense body of water gave me a feeling of insignificance.

It was a very long day and I ached from sitting on that metal roof. Deep thinking was the only thing I could do to make the time pass.

When we got to about twenty miles out of Centura, the fonapp on my hand comp lit up like a Christmas tree. I had over thirty voicemails from electrical customers, our lawyer, and the Department of Defense in Atlanta.

Finally, around seven, Wheeze reduced the throttle and aimed our 'Beast' into the shore. We borrowed the beach of one of the new log homes that were going up east of our property. Fortunately, it was unsold and vacant.

A smile broke out on Ben's face when we came onto dry land, and he gave me the thumbs up sign. After feeling safe enough to stretch out a bit, we gave each other pats on the back.

Many below deck personnel came out and rode outside when we entered our compound. Ben had called ahead to inform everyone. I noticed Marie, Diane, and the kids all heading for the machine shed.

After shutting off the motor, Wheeze and the rest of us got out to greet our loved ones. No one was interested in unloading anything.

When we saw Mary, Clyde's girlfriend, walk up, and kiss him smack on the mouth, we cheered.

Angie teased, "Hey you two, we got kids around here."

Mary blushed and they walked off arm in arm.

Marie walked up and kissed me, then pulled her head back and asked, "Did you find out?"

"I did. I have a lot to talk about but need a long shower first."

She smiled, "I like your beard."

"Really?"

"No, not really. Think you can take care of that too?"

I nodded. I picked up both my kids, hugged them hard, and we walked to the house.

"I didn't know if this homecoming would call for a party or not, Dan, so we didn't plan one," Marie informed me.

"Why don't we hold off a couple of weeks, I have some loose ends to tie up," I said.

I noticed that Frank Davis and Frank Miller were loading our special cargo into Davis' car for transport. The rest of us went home.

The next two weeks were a hectic mess. Al and I had to meet with Mr. Durham and several security people from the Defense Department to explain how that SOS transmission was sent. Then, we had to convince them that we were not going to pull a similar stunt. Also, Hightower wanted full transcripts of our expedition to be ready in case they tried to charge us with anything. We also discussed the ordinance to annex our property that the council did not pass and how it affected us. Captain Richardson and Mrs. Henderson wanted to be briefed also. I had to call my brother, who was in South America studying the ecosphere, and explain everything to him. Dr. Phillips wanted to know how his motor was and Dr. Principi wanted my graduate application. Finally, Ron wanted to tell me about all the new jobs we had. That was just day one.

The next day, and several after that, the U.S. Attorney's office wanted Al, Ben, Ms. Hightower, and I to go over everything again. Plus, I also had to call everyone who helped me and thank them.

Early one morning, Al Myers set me up on a vidcon with Bob Wilson at the nursing home in Mississippi. I didn't tell him about the expedition, but did say I found out the details about my parents. I then had my wife and kids get on camera with me and we all talked for a while. Of course, all of his nursing home friends joined him on camera there.

After two weeks, I figured everything was in place. On Saturday, I called Ron to tell him I needed a personal day and wouldn't be in to work.

When Clyde arrived at my doorstep, I said to Marie, "I'm going to give Clyde a ride to the base, stop at the hospital, then stop by and thank Mr. Greene."

"Okay, be careful," she responded.

We stopped at Mr. Greene's house first to thank him. His butler had this weekend off. He greeted us warmly at the door.

We took seats in his study, and I said, "Art, this is one of my partners, Clyde. We're on our way up to the base so I figured I'd stop by to thank you for helping me."

"Well, I didn't do that much, but I'm glad I could help. Did you find out about your parents?"

"Yes. They are deceased."

"Oh, I'm sorry, Dan. Did you find out how?"

"Yes. They were murdered."

"Really, by who?"

"Why, by you, Art."

He sat there with a stunned look on his face, and then said, "What? Where did you get a crazy idea like that?"

"You made a mistake, Art. You had the perfect crime going, and it would have succeeded if not for one tiny blunder."

"Do go on."

"We had the help of the Feds with all this. It is a long, complicated story. Do you have a few minutes? I think you do. We'll get back to my parents in a minute. I found a witness who said you were a good man, Art, and that you brought a lot of stuff up to Leap Frog to help with their operation. The Feds found an elderly retired supply sergeant who worked at the demolition warehouse at Fort Polk. My friend, Clyde, here served there while he was awaiting his discharge at that same warehouse. Well, they put this guy 'under the lights' and he 'sang like a bird'. It seems that you 'appropriated' a lot of stuff out of there, and illegally, by the way. One item was a laser rock drill. That's a mining tool, is it not? Leap Frog didn't have a mining license. The government would have objected to that, Art, not to mention the United Mine Workers Union.

"It seems that some federal precious metal storage sites were looted in that area. Clyde told me that the Feds thought it was done during the climate change and 'The Chaos' several centuries before. However, not so, you and Leo Gustav took it, didn't you?

"So, the authorities did a little checking around. First, your bogus Estuary Hydrofracturing Company in Guatemala turned out to be a company only on paper. They owned no property there, no equipment, and had no employees. Also, the alleged oil company in Argentina that bought it out doesn't even exist. The Guatemalan police raided the home of an Ernesto Gustav, younger brother of Leo. He's still alive. They found some of that gold there, Art. You and Leo Gustav drilled into the storage vaults, sent the gold to Ernesto, and he fenced it. Ernesto even sent you checks, written on the company account, to pay off your share and also fool the IRS. This explains how you bought this very nice house, doesn't it?

"Switching over to the flood, my witness also said you provided some pumps for the site. That got me thinking. Earlier in your career, you were assigned to New Orleans, right? Hmm, what does the Army Corps of Engineers do in New Orleans? That would be flood protection, right? I even have a copy of an article you coauthored entitled, 'The Cycles of Flooding in the Mississippi River Basin.' This is interesting. My witness also indicted that my Dad was working on a berm of some sort, just north of the site. Why the heck would they be putting in a berm up there? A berm sounds a lot like a dike to me. In fact, the Feds looked back at the historical satellite photos of the Old St. Louis site. They have an aerial picture taken in October 3055 that shows not only an earthen dike, but also one with steel reinforcement plates stuck into the ground on top. It's estimated to be eight to ten feet tall. You were very well aware that a ten-foot dike would not hold back that river in a flood, Art. My Dad knew it too, that is why you both got out of there long before spring flooding season.

"What is important, Art, is your responsibility. I was reading through the inspection parameters and you were responsible for assessing '… all earthen and other structures related to landscaping, foundations, roads, and especially flood protection.' Mr. Kline, area director, wanted you to pass that dike on your inspection report, didn't he? You knew that it would be practically useless in a big flood. You also knew that if no dike were erected, the company would be liable for not providing adequate protection for their employees. If one was built and you deemed it sound when it wasn't, you'd be liable. I have your final inspection report, Art, and nowhere in it do you mention a levee. A thousand people drowned in that flood, and the Feds have been trying to pin criminal negligence charges on someone for decades. With a report showing no dike there, you were off the hook."

Mr. Greene demanded, "I want to see those satellite photos."

"I'm sure your lawyer will get them during the discovery process. Now we're moving on to the important part. I found it interesting that you asked me about who made the SOS call that led to my rescue. You didn't ask me if they found my parents because you already knew they were dead.

"You did know my Dad, Art, that much is sure. We also found out that you got that UXU amphibious vehicle from the warehouse in Fort Polk. My Dad worked on it and even made a note in the maintenance log to tell you about the lubrication. Patrick O'Dea was on to your schemes, either about the gold or the floodwall or the stolen items. After he left with my family and I, Leo Gustav signed out a dune buggy indicating he was going up north to retrieve some chainsaws. Only he came by, picked you up, and you both followed my Dad. Things were turning out even better than expected. You two had my family out on the prairie with no witnesses around.

"However, O'Dea's route was a little erratic, was it not? You had some trouble tracking him. You finally caught up with him just about a hundred miles south of here. While a blizzard was approaching, you found him broken down and walking out on the prairie with his wife. That's when you shot them both. Figuring that the two little boys would die out there, you just left us and started the return trip."

"I did bring one photo with me."

I removed it from my shirt pocket, unfolded it, and handed it to him. "This is another one of those satellite pictures taken the day after my parents were killed. There's the dune buggy and there's two men standing next to it. This is about twenty miles southwest of where my parents lay. My gosh, Art, that looks a lot like you and Leo standing there, and you appear to be holding identical weapons. The Feds have an even more close-up photo showing that it is you two and the weapons are indeed identical. They were the conventional rifles issued by the military."

Mr. Greene didn't respond.

"A couple of days later, you had an accident in which Leo Gustav was killed. The impact was so hard he went through the windshield, but you survived, correct? This worked out great for you. You made sure you got everything out of the buggy that could place you there, and walked back to Old St. Louis.

"I met some people down near that area, Art, just a few weeks ago. They recall that time. A group of them found my parents, and then tracked you. They found the dune buggy, Leo Gustav's body, and the murder weapon. They were even convinced that old Leo was the killer. When I was there, they even gave me the gun to bring back with me.

"Well, seems the Feds got interested and they went down there, exhumed my parents' bodies, and even found the rifle slugs still in them, and guess what? A ballistics test showed that the bullets in them came from the gun I brought back, the one they found in Leo's dune buggy."

Mr. Greene perked up a little, "Looks like you got your killer. Maybe you should check your facts on those other two wild stories before you go accusing people." He started to stand up.

"How about you keep sitting," Clyde said sternly, and pulled his army fatigue shirt open to reveal his sidearm. "I'm awful good with this gun."

"I would do as he says, Art. Now, where were we? Well, something started bothering me about this single person theory. First, Leo Gustav was a conscientious objector in the military, wasn't he, Art? He couldn't just kill someone, could he? It would have been hard for him even when he had legal permission to do so, and you know what? After getting those slugs out of my parents, the Feds went over to pull that dune buggy out of the river. There wasn't much left of it, except the windshield. You see, my witnesses said old Leo went through the windshield, but failed to note that he went through on the passenger side. That's odd. Wouldn't someone else have had to be driving?

"And finally we get to the gun. You had yours issued to you at Fort Polk, right? We have the serial number. Leo bought his at a gun store in Alabama just before he left for his job at Leap Frog in Old St. Louis. We have that number too, and the bullets fired into my Mom and Dad were from the gun my friends found in the dune buggy."

Greene snarled, "You already said that! I turned mine in when I was discharged in '57."

"Yep, here at Thompson. The gun you turned in, Art, is long gone, recycled, but we did find the inventory the discharge clerk filled out at the time. Noting that it was the same kind of rifle you were issued at Fort Polk, he just wrote down the number and didn't check it. We did. It was the serial number of Leo's gun.

"It was your only mistake, Art. After the accident, you went back to the dune buggy to get your stuff, only you took the wrong gun."

Art Greene just sat there, staring at us. Then he rose from his chair. "Well, you guys are going to have to leave now. Thanks for sharing this crazy fantasy."

He walked to the foyer and we followed behind. Pulling open his front door, there stood the two MPs that had taken in Wheeze and I.

"Arthur Greene," one of them said, "We're placing you under arrest for the murder of Lilly and Patrick O'Dea, grand theft, theft of government property, vehicular homicide, and, well, this list is so long I'll read the rest later." He read him his rights while the other handcuffed him.

Mr. Greene stood, not saying a word. For a second, he seemed almost relieved.

After Clyde and I got in my truck, he said, "Kelley, remind me never to cross you. How do you feel?"

"Surprisingly, kind of sad. I thought I would be elated. Greene started serving his time when his wife died and his son turned bad. I don't think he had malice on his mind when he fudged that inspection report. While a Mississippi River flood was eminent, it could have skipped that spring, and then the site would be closed. I think he began to realize all that money he got in exchange for my parents' lives could not make him happy."

"Did you know all along that your dad was not part of a sinister government plot?"

"I didn't have any proof, but I highly doubted it. Ben watches too many spy movies. Captain Richardson assured me that that Air Force jet we saw was there for no other reason than a pilot logging some flight hours. Plus, Mr. Durham's enthusiasm to bring in the U.S. Attorney to develop a case against Green sealed it."

Clyde and I walked down the hall in the hospice wing of the military hospital only to see his girlfriend, Mary, come walking toward us. In order to avoid a public display of affection, the two just traded winks.

"We're here to see 'Mom', how is she doing?" I asked.

"Dan, she is terminal, you know?" Mary said.

"That's what she told me."

"She's pain free and already complaining about the food."

"So, can I see her?"

"Sure."

I left Clyde and Mary in the hall, while I went to 'Mom's room. I found her sitting by the window and looking out into the tree grove outside. "I hear you're complaining about the food."

She laughed, "Hi, Daniel."

"How are you feeling?"

"Really good. At least I can sleep at night. This medication is really something. If I would have known I'd feel this good, I would have started taking it years ago."

We laughed.

"I hope your ride up in the back of the 'Beast' was okay."

"It was fine. I actually took a nap when we were on the water. I wanted to be asleep if the darn thing sank. Did everything work out?"

"It did. We just wrapped things up. Thanks, also, for giving me Greene's rifle to bring back."

"The federal people were here yesterday to take my statement, since I may not be around for any trial. Oh, your lovely wife came to visit me one morning. How did you land someone that nice?"

"To this day I have no idea how.

I can't stay long. Anyway, I wanted to tell you that I'm bringing her and the kids up tomorrow. We're going to let them terrorize you for a while."

"I'd like to meet Patrick's grandchildren."

We hugged and then I departed.

When Clyde and I pulled into my driveway, we noticed Bo Schlitz standing in our campsite next to the bunkhouse talking to Corky Wall. He was clean-shaven and appeared to have slimmed down some. I rushed over there to greet him.

"Did you pull a jailbreak?" I asked

"No, just a weekend pass."

We shook hands.

"The doc said maybe one more week and he'll discharge me. Cork tells me you guys have been awful busy."

"Yeah. I want to thank you, Bo, for giving us a few clues."

"That's what Cork said, but I don't really know how I helped."

"You have your ways. Anyway, I've been thinking that since I am pretty busy now, you might want to help me with my electrical business. I need someone to prepare work sites, set up, stuff like that."

Bo smiled, "That's funny, because it's my second job offer today. Dr. Myers wants me to be a research assistant, to help him with math stuff. Dan, I don't know the first thing about math and I'd probably electrocute myself working with you. Thanks for the offer, but I think I'll just keep working for the LLC. I like tending to the garden and the farm animals."

Late that afternoon, we had our long overdue campfire party. We began early to let my kids attend. Corky Wall cooked up a great vegetarian ragout. Of course, some of us had plastic bags containing pemmican in our pockets to dump in our bowls when no one was looking.

Everyone attended; even Frank Davis brought Ms. Hightower. It was so odd to see those two arm-in-arm.

When our partners were busy with cleanup detail, she leaned over to me and said quietly, "You know, Dan, confronting Greene like that was probably the dumbest thing you've ever done."

"I know. It was something I just had to do."

"Also, that charge for murdering your parents has a lot of holes in it. The blizzard prevented getting any satfotos of him in the act, and Gustav could have made the same mistake of grabbing the wrong rifle when it came time to shoot them. You have no live witnesses."

"I know, I was told all that. However, the U.S. Attorney said the charge of stealing that gold was almost airtight. We have a documentation trail and a live witness."

"Yeah, there's enough there to assure he'll be in prison for the rest of his life. I am very proud of you. I don't think I could have figured out that series of events, even on my best day."

"I cheated a little. I wasn't bound by the same rules you or Dr. Myers are. I had to take some leaps of faith. By the way, Ms. Hightower, may I ask you a personal question?"

She smiled. "Okay, just this once."

"What's your first name?"

She laughed. "Christine. Don't ever call me that."

After finishing up our meals, Tom Pine said so everyone could hear, "Dan, we've just completed another great adventure. Do you have anything to say in summary of it all?"

I held on to little Patrick while I spoke, "First, thank you all for helping me with this. Thank you for always helping me. To start off, I want to thank all the little people." I smiled, looking at Angie.

"I knew it!" Angie said smiling and shaking her head. "I knew he couldn't waste one whole speech without giving me a shot. He can't help it, but I'm 'Little Woman, Big Fist' now, so watch it."

I went on, "You know, all these years I felt this mystery was preventing me from moving on with my life. I used to wake up in the morning and felt unfocused and unsure about what direction I wanted my life to go. Now that I have it all worked out, guess what? I still wake up unfocused and unsure, and it's because I'm an unfocused and unsure person. I like a lot of different things. I'm eclectic, so sue me.

"Most importantly, I remember I would always ask people, 'was my Dad a good man?' I heard he was, thank goodness, but how bad can a man who sang to cows be? I soon realized, however, that didn't matter. It didn't matter if he was a good man or not; it's only important if I am. I have three good reasons sitting next to me here that tell me I have to be."

I received the good-natured 'boos' after my speech, of course. Our Saturday night discussion then continued, but it was different this time. That night we talked about each of our plans and goals. Ben talked about where our LLC was going and how we could better serve the community.

Up until then, we were consumed with these mysterious ancestors of ours. We had put too much emphasis on genetics. That night we realized that the kind of people we were, we became in that orphanage. We built trusts and friendships there. We became competent there. Our family was here, right here, sitting around this campfire. There was no other, and we had done a pretty good job with raising ourselves.

Later in the evening, my handcomp buzzed.

Marie picked it up, and then handed it to me. "It's Captain Richardson."

I took it. "Hello, Commodore."

"I'll have you know," his voice came out of the device, "that I'm now Rear Admiral Richardson and that I shall be treated with the proper respect."

"Hey, great. They finally gave it to you? Are you going to stay in the Navy now and drive them all crazy?"

"No, I think it's mainly ceremonial. They must have felt bad for me, leaving me up at Thompson all these years. They didn't even tell me until after I submitted my retirement application. At least I'll have the title of retired admiral. My official date is next Friday and they're having a party for me."

"Oh, so you called to invite us all to the party, right?"

"Heck no. I don't want a bunch of delinquent orphans there; I have a reputation to uphold." He laughed. "However, I just wanted you to know that everything went okay down South."

"Thank you, Admiral, for sending down those people in that helicopter to look at my parents and that dune buggy."

"Sure. I just wanted you to know that the forensic pathologist did his job, and then put your folks back where they were. They are resting there."

"Thanks."

"Oh, Dan. There is something bothering me. You gave me a vague indication that there were some people living out there. The chopper commander told me he didn't see anybody or any indication of someone around the area."

"Probably not. They are hard to see unless you know exactly where to look."

ABOUT THE AUTHOR

David J. Kirk, an honorable discharged veteran of the United States Navy, earned his master's degree in personality psychology from Rhode Island College. He worked as a counselor and human resources manager. David then became an instructor at Rasmussen College in Fargo where he taught psychology and sociology for four years. An avid writer since 16 years old, he first published *Particular Stones* with Martin Sisters Publishing in 2011. Besides *Cornerstones,* David has many other works in progress. He lives with his wife, Dawne, in Logansport, Indiana.

www.ingramcontent.com/pod-product-compliance
Lightning Source LLC
Chambersburg PA
CBHW071140260626
47162CB00003B/860